W9-BXW-544

STORY AND ART BY
NORIYUKI KONISHI

ORIGINAL CONCEPT AND SUPERVISED BY LEVEL-5 INC.

YO-KAI WATCH™

Volume 12

BASHFUL YO-KAI MR. BLUE-SHY

VIZ Media Edition

Story and Art by Noriyuki Konishi
Original Concept and Supervised by LEVEL-5 Inc.

Translation/Tetsuichiro Miyaki
English Adaptation/Aubrey Sitterson
Lettering/John Hunt
Design/Shawn Carrico

YO-KAI WATCH Vol. 12
by Noriyuki KONISHI
© 2013 Noriyuki KONISHI
©LEVEL-5 Inc.
Original Concept and Supervised by LEVEL-5 Inc.
All rights reserved.
Original Japanese edition published by SHOGAKUKAN.
English translation rights in the United States of America, Canada, the United Kingdom, Ireland, Australia and New Zealand arranged with SHOGAKUKAN.

The stories, characters and incidents mentioned in this publication are entirely fictional.

No portion of this book may be reproduced or transmitted in any form or by any means without written permission from the copyright holders.

Printed in the U.S.A.

Published by VIZ Media, LLC
P.O. Box 77010
San Francisco, CA 94107

10 9 8 7 6 5 4 3 2 1
First printing, September 2019

STORY AND ART BY
NORIYUKI KONISHI

ORIGINAL CONCEPT AND SUPERVISED BY LEVEL-5 INC.

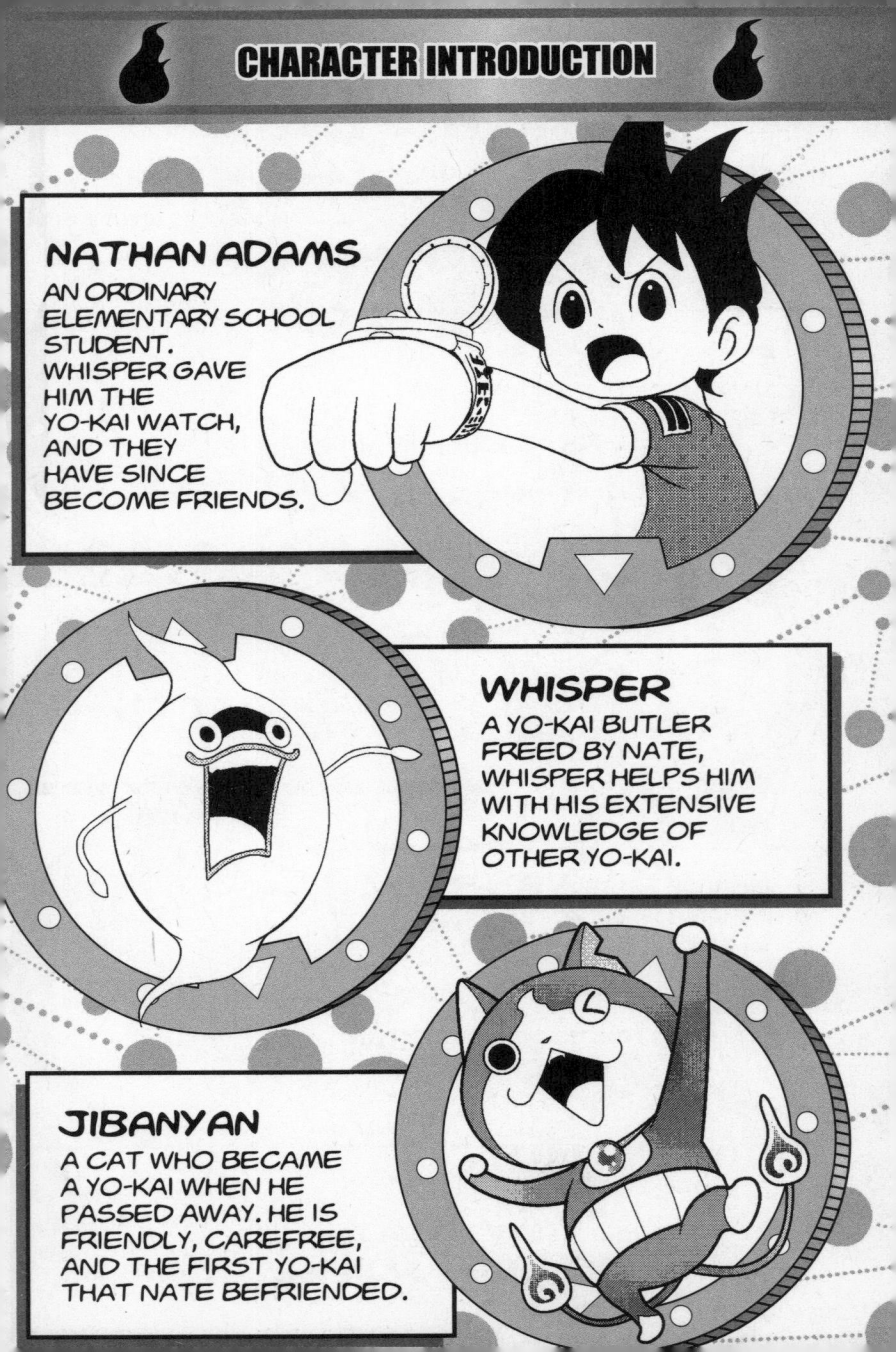
CHARACTER INTRODUCTION
NATHAN ADAMS
AN ORDINARY ELEMENTARY SCHOOL STUDENT. WHISPER GAVE HIM THE YO-KAI WATCH, AND THEY HAVE SINCE BECOME FRIENDS.
WHISPER
A YO-KAI BUTLER FREED BY NATE, WHISPER HELPS HIM WITH HIS EXTENSIVE KNOWLEDGE OF OTHER YO-KAI.
JIBANYAN
A CAT WHO BECAME A YO-KAI WHEN HE PASSED AWAY. HE IS FRIENDLY, CAREFREE, AND THE FIRST YO-KAI THAT NATE BEFRIENDED.

BARNABY BERNSTEIN
NATE'S CLASSMATE.
NICKNAME: BEAR.
CAN BE MISCHIEVOUS.
EDWARD ARCHER
NATE'S CLASSMATE.
NICKNAME: EDDIE.
ALWAYS WEARS HEADPHONES.
USAPYON
A RABBIT-LIKE YO-KAI IN A SPACESUIT. HE CAME FROM THE COUNTRY OF BBQ.
HAILEY ANNE THOMAS
A FIFTH GRADER WHO IS A SELF-PROCLAIMED SUPERFAN OF ALIENS AND SAILOR CUTIES.
TOMNYAN
A MYSTERIOUS YO-KAI WHO ALSO COMES FROM THE COUNTRY OF BBQ. HE SEEMS TO HAVE AN ULTERIOR MOTIVE...

TABLE OF CONTENTS

Chapter 110: Bashful Yo-kai Mr. Blue-Shy 7

Chapter 111: Hungry Yo-kai Hungramps 30

Chapter 112: Rich Yo-kai Flash T. Cash 49

Chapter 113: Snap Decision Yo-kai Decidevible 59

Chapter 114: Take a Break Yo-kai Re-Q-Perate 72

Chapter 115: Klutz Yo-kai Clodzilla 89

Chapter 116: Unintentional Yo-kai Push Pup 97

Chapter 117: On the Edge Yo-kai Humtea Jumtea 105

Chapter 118: Bath Lover Yo-kai Lil Blue Bathing Hood ... 113

Chapter 119: Unpredictable Yo-kai Unbelievaboy! 121

Chapter 120: Herbivore Yo-kai Herbiboy 129

Chapter 121: Listening Yo-kai Naahndi 137

Chapter 122: Witch Girl Yo-kai Maginyan 145

Chapter 123: No-Good Yo-kai Nummskull 153

Chapter 124: Kickback Yo-kai Ulteria 161

CHAPTER 110: BASHFUL YO-KAI MR. BLUE-SHY

SURE! ♪
HEY KATIE! WANT TO WALK HOME TOGETHER? ♪
DING DINGDING DING DING
BYE ♪
SEE YOU LATER! ♪
...
...
YEAH? W-W-WHAT'S UP?
UMM... NATE...?

THIS ISN'T EXACTLY WALKING HOME TOGETHER."
WHY ARE YOU ALL THE WAY BACK THERE?
HEH-HEH-HEH. ♪
WHAT? BUT WALKING HOME TOGETHER WAS YOUR IDEA!
W-W-WELL... I'M JUST FEELING A LITTLE... SHY...TO BE WALKING WITH YOU. ♪

BASHFUL BASHFUL
YEAH...I KNOW... ♪
I'LL WALK THE REST OF THE WAY BY MYSELF. TALK TO YOU LATER! ♪
SOMETIMES YOU GET TO TALKING TO YOURSELF AND YOUR WHOLE PERSONALITY CHANGES...IT LOOKS LIKE IT'S ONE OF THOSE DAYS, NATE. ♪
REALLY? WE TALK TO EACH OTHER ALL THE TIME THOUGH!
HEH HEH
IT'S JUST. TALKING TO YOU IS A LITTLE.. EMBARAS SING... ♪
HEH
HEH

WHAAAA
WHAT WAS I JUST DOING?!
HUH?
WHERE DID HE GO...?
HUH? WHISPER?
WHISPER! WHY DIDN'T YOU SAY ANY-THING?!
AHHHHH!
THIS WAS MY BIG CHANCE TO TALK TO HER ALONE!
DO YOU SEE ANY YO-KAI?
AH! THERE YOU ARE, WHISPER!
AWAASH
COULD IT BE A YO-KAI?!
WHY DO I FEEL LIKE SOME-ONE'S WATCHING ME?
SHFF
SHFF
...

WHAT?! YOU'RE NOT WHISPER! YOUR HEAD JUST LOOKS LIKE HIS!
WHO ARE YOU?!
WELL THEN, GOOD-BYE.
SWIP
EH...
I NEVER THOUGHT I'D MEET A HUMAN WHO CAN SEE YO-KAI... ♪
BASHFUL
BASHFUL
AW SHUCKS... I'M NOBODY REALLY... ♪

HOLD IT RIGHT THERE!
CHAK
THUNGK
HUURGH!
GASP
YOU MUST BE THE REASON I WAS ACTING SO WEIRD!
OOOOH...
HEH HEH HEH... ♪ OH IT WAS NOTHING. ♪
STOP BLUSHING! I'M NOT COMPLI-MENTING YOU!
OH, REALLY? GUESS I GOT MIXED UP. ♪ HEHEHEH. ♪
BASHFUL BASHFUL
IT'S STILL BLUSH-ING!
MY NAME IS, EH... EH...
MR BLUE-SHY. ANYONE INSPIRITED BY ME BECOMES UM... UM...
THEY BECOME SHY, RIGHT?
HAT ?

BASHFUL
BASHFUL
YOU'VE HEARD OF ME? REALLY?
I'VE NEVER HEARD OF HIM, BUT IT WASN'T HARD TO FIGURE OUT!
BASHFUL YO-KAI
MR. BLUE-SHY
WHISPER!
CHEEKY
NATE! I'M OVER HERE...!
WHO'S WHISPER?
WHERE'S WHISPER? WHAT DID YOU DO WITH HIM?
SHUT
...
I'VE ALREADY FIGURED IT OUT. STOP WASTING TIME AND COME OUT HERE.
I JUST...I FEEL TOO EMBARRASSED TO SHOW MYSELF.. DON'T KNOW WHY...

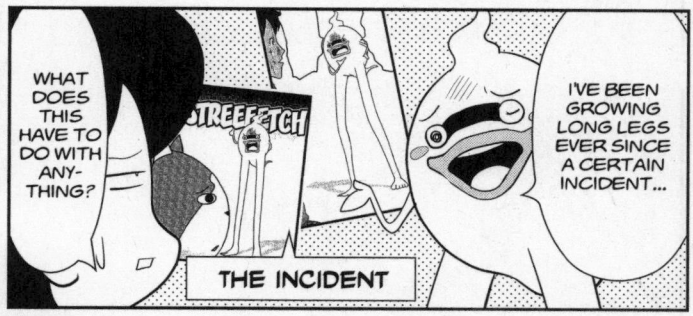

THAT YOU REALIZED YOU LOOK ABSURD!!

I LOOKED GROSS ?!
WHAT?
BAAAAM
SHOCK
HOW COULD YOU MAKE MY MASTER LOOK SO GROSS IN FRONT OF A GIRL?!

YUP! THE ENTIRE THING!
BUT KATIE STILL SAW ME, RIGHT?
BAAM
UGH
...I CLOSED MY EYES AND STOPPED WATCHING!

BUT DON'T WORRY, IN ORDER TO SPARE YOU SOME EMBARRASS-MENT...
IT WAS ABSOLUTELY AWFUL!
...

YOU'RE MY BUTLER, RIGHT?! WHY DIDN'T YOU STOP THIS YO-KAI FROM INSPIRITING ME?!
BASHFUL
BASHFUL
MY LEGS STARTED TO GROW AND...I JUST GOT SO EMBARRASSED...
BUT YOUR MASTER WAS BEING EVEN MORE EMBARRASSED!
FIDGET FIDGET
BYE.
...
GRRRRR...! JUST DRIVING YOU AWAY ISN'T ENOUGH!
!!
WOOSH
YO-KAI MEDAL! DO YOUR THING!
KRRKT
CALLING...
JIBANYAN!
WNNNNOOO

VRRRN...
...

KR-R-RCH
WHISPER! PULL HIM OUT!
I'M ON IT!
WHAT?! YOU'RE STUCK?!

WE'RE TRYING TO HELP YOU OUT!
CHOP!
CHOP!
STOP IT! DON'T TOUCH ME!
...HIS FAULT?!
COULD IT BE...
STREEEETCH
STREEEETCH
NOOOOOO! I DON'T WANT TO APPEAR IN THIS CHAPTER! I'M TOO EMBARRASSED!
HMM?
THAT WAS UNCALLED FOR!
SHOUPT
MEEOOW!
HE'S OUT!

YOU'RE STILL SUFFERING FROM "THE INCIDENT" TOO?!

BAAAM

DON'T LOOK AT ME!

THIS IS SO EMBARRASSING!!

SHOOM!

I'LL WORRY FOREVER FOR THIS!

LOOK AT HEAD!

GRRRRRRRR!
!!!
I WON'T FORGIVE ANYONE WHO GIVES NATE TROUBLE!
THAT SNAPPED HIM OUT OF IT!
PAWS OF FURY!

FWOO
FWOO
FWOO
HEH HEH HEH... YOUR ATTACKS CAN'T HARM MY FLIMSY BODY.
I MIGHT BE BASHFUL. I MIGHT LOOK WEAK...
...BUT DON'T UNDER-ESTIMATE ME!
!!
BASHFUL PUNCH!

SHF
WHAT?!
AHHH... I JUST CAN'T DO IT! I'M TOO EMBAR-RASSED TO GET INTO A FIGHT!
THUNGKT
THIS DOESN'T MAKE ANY SENSE!
ONE MORE TIME...
NOW I KNOW THAT YOUR HEAD IS SOLID!
I DIDN'T EVEN SEE WHAT HAPPENED!
HEE-HEE... HOW EMBAR-RASSING...

NO MATTER HOW MANY TIMES YOU TRY...YOU'LL NEVER HIT ME! ♪
PAWS OF FURY!
YEAH? WELL, I'M NOT TRYING TO HIT YOU!
?!
WHAT?! I CAN'T MOVE!
GOTCHA! ♪
GLOMPT
HUUURGH!
YOU WERE AIMING FOR MY SCARF!
THAT'S A SCARF ?!
I'LL JUST TAKE IT OFF...!
HUP!
TUG

TAKE THAT!
THUNGK!

HNNGH
I GIVE UP...

SO I PROTECT MYSELF BY BEING BASHFUL...
AND I'D BE SO EMBARRASSED IF I TRIED AND STILL FAILED...
I'VE NEVER HAD MUCH CONFI-DENCE IN MYSELF...

SO YOU DID ABAN-DON ME!
I ABANDONED MY MASTER TODAY BECAUSE I DIDN'T HAVE THE COURAGE TO TAKE ACTION. ♪
I UNDERSTAND... IT'S HARD TO KNOW WHAT TO DO WHEN YOU DON'T HAVE ANY CONFIDENCE.

FRIENDS...
JIBANYAN...
BUT I WAS ABLE TO MUSTER MY COURAGE BECAUSE I WANTED TO HELP MY FRIEND. ♪
MEOW. ♪ I WAS ABOUT TO ABANDON HIM TOO.
THAT WAS HIS REAL MOTIVATION...
PRK PRK
BASHFUL, BASHFUL
UHH, NATE... BY THE WAY... COULD YOU HURRY UP AND CALL FURGUS...?
..TO EVEN ACTUALLY TALK WITH ME. ♪
YOU GUYS ARE THE FIRST...
O-OKAY...
ANYWAY, LIKE YOU JUST HEARD,... EVERYONE KNOWS THAT FEELING. YOU SHOULD TRY TO HAVE A LITTLE MORE CONFIDENCE FROM NOW ON!
WELL...
I SEE...
I'M SO BASHFUL THAT I'VE NEVER REALLY HAD ANY FRIENDS...

IF YOU WOULDN'T MIND YOUR FIRST FRIEND BEING A HUMAN...
...I'LL BE YOUR FRIEND!
!!!

REALLY? I THOUGHT YOU DIDN'T LIKE ME...!
THAT WAS BEFORE I GOT TO KNOW YOU! ♪

...

AND IT'S ONLY NATURAL TO TRY AND HELP SOMEONE STRUGGLING WITH SELF-CONFIDENCE!

SHUK
THANK YOU! ♪

I SHOULD MUSTER MY COURAGE AND JUMP INTO HIS ARMS!
I'VE NEVER MET SOMEONE WHO COULD SAY SOMETHING SO SINCERE WITHOUT BEING EMBAR-RASSED!

THUNGK

URRGH!

OOOF!

NATE ADAMS'S CURRENT NUMBER OF YO-KAI FRIENDS: 71

CHAPTER 111: HUNGRY YO-KAI HUNGRAMPS

HEY! HEY, HEY, HEY, HEY, HEY!
HEY! HEY, HEY, HEY, HEY, HEY, HEY!
HEY, HEY!
HEY, HEY!
HEY, HEY!
HEY, HEY!
HEEEEEEEEY!
HEY!!!

I TOLD YOU THAT I WAS AN IMPORTANT CHARACTER, DIDN'T I?!
WHY HAVEN'T I BEEN IN THIS MANGA LATELY?!
AND SO, IN THIS CHAPTER ...
RAMBLE
YOU'VE ALWAYS BEEN A STAR IN MY EYES!
YO-KAI WATCH
8
YOU MEAN I'M ALREADY A STAR?
BUT I'VE ALREADY DONE THAT...!
HMM ...
MAYBE THEY'RE SAVING YOU FOR ONE OF THOSE ICONIC SCENES WHERE A CHARACTER RUSHES BACK IN TO SAVE THEIR FRIENDS! ♪
ARRRRRRGH!!
NO NO ...

BUT...
I, USAPYON, AM THE MAIN CHARACTER!
YOU MONSTER! YOU MUST BE A HEARTLESS YO-KAI!
WHAAAA
THAT'S SO COLD AND CALLOUS!
YOU SHOULD GO BACK TO BBQ.
SNIFF
WHAT SHOULD I DO NOW...?
NOW THAT I FINISHED MY ROCKET... THERE'S NOTHING LEFT FOR ME TO DO.
WE'LL SOLVE ANY PROBLEM!
INTRODUCING...
OOOH! IT'S YOUR WAY OF GIVING BACK! ♪
SO I'M GOING TO TRACK THEM DOWN AND HELP THEM!
I BET THERE ARE OTHER YO-KAI THAT ARE IN TROUBLE, JUST LIKE I WAS!
SO I'VE MADE A DECISION ...
I'VE GROWN REALLY FOND OF THIS PLACE, AND OF YOU AND NATE TOO!

...THE HAPYON DETECTIVE AGENCY!!
THAT SOUNDS FUN! ♪
YES! THERE'S A POOR ELEMENTARY SCHOOL GIRL WHO IS ABOUT TO GET FORCED INTO CHILD LABOR! SOMEONE HELP ME!
WELL THEN... LET'S SEE WHO'S IN TROUBLE!
HMMM
WHAAA
WAIT A MINUTE...! WAIT A MINUTE! IS THE "HA" PART SUPPOSE TO BE ME??!
OH? THAT'S ...
!!
RABBLE
RABBLE
WHAT'S THIS? THAT CONVENIENCE STORE HAS SUCH A LONG LINE!
LISTEN TO ME!

BUT PEOPLE CUT IN LINE AND AREN'T LETTING HIM GET INSIDE!
EVERYMART
YO-KAI WATCH VOLS. 1-12 NOW AVAILABLE!
HELP WANTED!
THERE'S A CONFUSED OLD MAN STANDING NEARBY!
WE HAVE TO REPAY OUR DEBT TO HIM!
OH! YOU'RE RIGHT!
YES!
THAT'S THE OLD MAN WHO HELPED US WHEN WE WERE LOOKING FOR DOCTOR HUGHLY!
HUH?
!
HEY... WHAT?!
YOU'RE TAKING A ROCKET?! HE'S JUST DOWN THE BLOCK!
THE MAIN CHARACTER SHOULD ALWAYS MAKE A BIG ENTRANCE!
GWOOO
HANG ON, OLD MAN! I'M ON MY WAY!

I THOUGHT YOU WERE GOING TO HELP HIM...
GET OUT OF THE WAY, OLD MAN! QUICKLY!
I'M ALL OUT OF BATTERIES I CAN'T CONTROL THE ROCKET!
I CAN'T STOP! HELP MEEEEE!
BLINK
?
PLEASE DON'T STOP ME!
WOW! WHEN DID YOU BEFRIEND NOWAY?!
FOR GOD'S SAKE! NOWAY, PLEASE!
NOOOO WAAAY!
DON'T STOP THAT ROCKET!
NOOO WAAAY!
HE REFUSES TO DO FAVORS FOR YOU, SO HE'LL HELP YOU IF YOU ASK HIM TO DO THE OPPOSITE.

HE'S TOO FAR AWAY! THERE'S NO WAY HE CAN HELP ME!
HUFF HUFF
Nooo waaay...
You can do it
CLOMPT CLOMPT
I HAVE NO CHOICE ...
WHAT? WHAT DID YOU SAY?
AGGGH! THE OLD MAN'S JUST STANDING THERE!
PLIPT
I DON'T WANT TO HURT ANYONE!
WHAT ?!
HUUUH?
SELF-DESTRUCT!

WOOOSH
YOU IDIOT!
NOOOO! WITHOUT ANY BATTERIES I CAN'T EVEN SELF-DISTRUCT!
NO! PLEASE! OUT OF MY WAY!
A-THOOM
NOOOO WARDY!
NO-WAY!
WHERE DID YOU COME FROM?
PHEE-EEW ...

THAT WAS CLOSE.
NATE!
NATE MUST HAVE SUMMONED HIM! ♪
WERE YOU WAITING IN THAT LINE TOO?
VNNNN
THANKS A LOT...
NOWAY, COULD YOU PUT ME DOWN SLOWLY–
OH NO...
NOOO WAAAY!
WOOSH
OH NOO-OOO!
HE DOES THE OPPOSITE OF WHAT YOU TELL HIM.
DOOOM
AIYEEE!

HNNNGH
AND YOU THINK YOU'RE THE MAIN CHARACTER?
SIZZLE
SIZZLE
THIS IS HUNGRY YO-KAI HUNGRAMPS.
I WAS TOO HUNGRY TO EVEN THINK ABOUT IT!
...I DIDN'T REALIZE IT WAS BECAUSE OF A YO-KAI!
I SUDDENLY GOT REALLY HUNGRY. BUT THERE WAS A HUGE LINE AT THE CONVENIENCE STORE...
NATE!
WHAT ARE YOU DOING HERE?
NOWA DON'T LEAVE
NOOO WAAAY ...
Thanks!
LUCKY ME! ♪
OOH, A YO-KAI MEDAL!
PLEASE ACCEPT THIS!
AS A TOKEN OF THANKS...
YOUNG BOY AND GIRL, THANK YOU FOR HELPING ME!
SHF
SHF
?
HUNGRY YO-KAI
HUNGRAMPS

HE'S LIKE A REAL GRAND-FATHER...
GO TREAT YOUR-SELF TO SOME-THING NICE!
I... THANK YOU...
WAIT... IT'S MONEY...?
100
GRRUMBLE
GRRUMBLE
GRRUMBLE
GRRUMBLE
BUT YOU'RE SO HUNGRY! PLEASE USE IT TO GET YOURSELF SOMETHING TO EAT!
USE IT TO BUY YOURSELF A SNACK...
?
IT'S OKAY! I LIKE BEING HUNGRY IN FRONT OF THIS STORE.

MY HUNGER BRINGS BACK THOSE SWEET MEMORIES...
EVERYMART
MY GRANDDAUGHTER AND I WOULD BUY LUNCH AND SNACKS HERE BACK WHEN I WAS STILL HUMAN...

...PULLING MY ARM WITH A SMILE ON HER FACE!
HURRY, GRANDPA! HURRY! ♪
I CAN ALMOST SEE HER NOW...

WE CAN'T HELP BUT WORRY!
GRRUMBLE
GRRUUMMBLE
GRUMBLE
SO DON'T WORRY ABOUT ME! GO GET YOURSELF SOME-THING TO EAT.
GRRUMBLE

WELL, YO-KAI CAN'T STARVE...
...AND HE'S HELPING THE STORE DO GREAT BUSINESS, SO WHAT'S THE HARM?
I guess you're right!
Thank you!
LET'S GO HOME AND EAT IT TOGETHER, GRANDPA!
...
MAYBE WE CAN EAT SOMETHING TOGETHER WHEN WE'RE ACTUALLY HUNGRY! ♪
Good idea!
PLEASE, IN EXCHANGE FOR WHAT YOU'VE GIVEN ME...
SHUFF
OOH. ♪ THIS TIME T'S FOR REAL!
YOU'VE HELPED ME RECALL A NEW MEMORY!
?

NATE ADAMS'S CURRENT NUMBER OF YO-KAI FRIENDS: 72

WHAT A COLOSSAL FAILURE!
I'M THE MAIN CHARACTER, BUT I DIDN'T EVEN HELP!
HE'S NOT DEPRESSED AT ALL!
OH WELL! ♪ ARE THERE ANY OTHER YO-KAI IN NEED OF HELP? ♪
HE WAS SO EXCITED TO HELP...I FEEL BAD FOR HIM...
FWUMPT
HEY! WHAT'S WRONG?!
YO-KAI!
HMM?
KRCH
SHUP...
URGH ...
JUST HOLD ON!
GRRUMBLE
WHAT?! IT'S BECAUSE OF THAT OLD MAN!
I'M SO... HUNGRY...

AIYEEEE!! A MONSTER!
WHAAA
GRRRRRRRW
THAT'S SO...
STAGGER
LOOK AT YOUR-SELF!
DID YOU JUST CALL ME A MONSTER ?!

SLASH
WHAAAAT?!
AIYEEE?!
...RUDE OF YOU!
I'M GOING...
YOU WANT A DUEL, HUH? BRING IT ON!
KRCH
THERE'S NO ROOM IN THIS TOWN FOR DANGEROUS GUYS LIKE YOU!
I'M GLAD HE'S OKAY!
WHAT ARE YOU TALKING ABOUT?! YOU ATTACKED ME OUT OF NOWHERE!
I CANNOT FORGIVE THOSE WHO DISRESPECT ME!

SWAASH
I THINK HE GOT TO YOU FIRST!
...TO BLAST YOU APART!
TWITCH
TWITCH
WAIT ...!
ARE YOU READY?
A TRUE DUEL CONTINUES UNTIL THE VERY END!
GRRRRRR...

CHAPTER 112: RICH YO-KAI FLASH T. CASH

FWUMP
...
I'M... SO...
...HUN... GRY...
HUH?
HNNGH
FWOO...
DUEL COM-PLETE!
HE STARVED!
FWAAA
PHEEW
I FEEL BAD, BUT AT LEAST YOU'RE OKAY, USAPYON...
YOU TOO?!

SHE HEALS WOUNDS BY LICKING THEM.
SLUUSH SLUUSH
LICK LICK LICK
!
Here!
AND THIS IS FOR YOU...
LICKETY-LICK. ♪
TONGUS!
TONGUS
THAT WAS DELI-CIOUS!
HUN-GRAMPS' MONEY CAME IN HANDY!
MUNCH MUNCH CHOMP CHOMP MUNCH MUNCH
THANK YOU SO MUCH!
A RICE BALL!
!!!
CALM DOWN, USA-PYON!
I'VE HAD JUST ABOUT ENOUGH!
...
!
GRRR-RRR! HOW DARE YOU!
THUNCK
WOW..., SO THAT'S HOW YOU ACTUALLY LOOK! ♪
I FEEL GREAT!
SAMURAI YO-KAI
LAST NYANMURAI

THIS IS UNACCEPTABLE!
I'M THE MAIN CHARACTER HERE! HOW DARE YOU TAKE MY SPOT ON THE COVER OF THE VOLUME!
妖怪ウォッチ
12
THAT'S WHY YOU'RE MAD?! HE JUST CUT YOU IN HALF!
FOR THE GIRLS' SAKE, I SHALL FORGIVE YOU JUST THIS ONCE. BUT DON'T LET ME CATCH YOU BEING DISRESPECTFUL AGAIN!
HE'S NOT EVEN LISTENING TO ME!
THEN PLEASE... FORGIVE USAPYON!
THANK YOU VERY MUCH. I OWE YOU A DEBT OF GRATITUDE FOR THE RICE BALL.

HE'S NOT EVEN LISTEN-ING!
I'M GONNA DO IT!
ALL RIGHT! IT'S TIME TO OFFICIALLY OPEN THE HAPYON DETECTIVE AGENCY!
DON'T FORGET BATTERIES FOR YOUR CONTROLLER!
I NEED TO REPAIR MY ROCKET SO I CAN MAKE A GRAND ENTRANCE!
BUT FIRST THINGS FIRST...
No! Please!
KRRCHK
THAT'S IT! I'M GOING TO SLICE HIM APART AGAIN!
IF YOU THINK ABOUT IT, IT'S CLEAR WHAT'S HAPPEN-ING.
WOW! AMAZ-ING!
LOOK! MONEY'S FALLING FROM THE SKY!
YES, I SEE!
UH-HUH!
HUH?
FWOO
FWOO
WOW...IT'S REALLY BUSTED UP. I DON'T HAVE ENOUGH MONEY...
AW, MAN...

HE'S OB-SESSED WITH WEALTH ...
NO! IT'S A YO-KAI!
SLAP
KRRCH KRRCH
IT'S MAGIC!
YEE-HAW!
KRRCH KRRCH

MWA HA HA. ♪
MWA HA HA. ♪

FAAASH...
HMM.

SOOOO MUCH MONEY! ♪ I'VE GOT MONEY TO BURN! ♪ MADE IT RAIN MONEY IN BBQ NOW I'M DOING IT AGAAAAAAAIN! ♪ JUST PICK IT UP! ♪ GO AHEAD AND TAKE IT! ♪
THEN ...

WADS OF MONEY! TONS OF MONEY! FLASH T. CASH! ♪
FWOOSH FWOOSH
RICH MAN! MAKE IT RAIN FLASH T. CASH! ♪
THERE HE IS! BUT WHAT A WEIRD SONG...

THIS IS LUDI-CROUS!
SHOOSH
MWA HAHA MWA HAHA
...REVERE ME! WORSHIP ME! GROVEL AT MY FEEEEEEET! ♪
SHOOSH
I THINK I CAN GUESS WHAT IT IS...
THERE IS ONE WORD... THAT I HATE... MORE THAN ANY OTHER WORD...
PRMBBLE
THAT'S TERRIBLE! IT'S GROSS! AND CHEAP!
BOO!
BOO!
HE'S RIGHT! DO YOU REALLY THINK YOU CAN JUST BUY PEOPLE'S AFFECTION ?!
WHY ARE YOU HIDING BEHIND ME...?
HA HA HA!
WHOA, HE'S REALLY ANGRY!
LITTLE GIRL, LET ME TELL YOU ONE THING!
GRRR
CHEAP...? DID YOU... JUST CALL ME... CHEAP?!

MISERLYYYYY!
AHHHH
IT'S NOT CHEAP? THEN WHY IS HE SO ANGRY?!
I AM NOT SOME CREEP WHO WANTS TO BUY POPULARITY WITH MONEY!
I JUST THROW MONEY AROUND TO SHOW EVERYONE HOW WONDERFUL I AM! THAT WAY EVERYONE KNOWS TO ADORE ME!
THAT'S STILL AWFUL. AND HE SURE TALKS A LOT...
"MONEY ISN'T EVERY-THING."
THAT'S JUST A LOUSY EXCUSE FROM PEOPLE WHO DON'T HAVE...
WHEN PEOPLE CAN'T APPRE-CIATE THAT...
...IT'S JUST SOUR GRAPES! THEY'RE JEALOUS OF ME!
SO I JUST SPEND MORE MONEY! I USE IT TO CRUSH THEM! AND IF THEY STILL WON'T BOW DOWN TO ME, I WIPE THEM OUT OF EXISTENCE!

...MON-AIEE-EEE!
AA SH
ARRRRRRGH!
D-D-DIDN'T MEAN IT?!
I'M SORRY...I DIDN'T MEAN IT. I JUST... COULDN'T HELP MYSELF.
AH!
ONLY COWARDS BASE THEIR SELF-WORTH ON MONEY!
LET THIS BE A LESSON TO YOU!
TWITCH TWITCH
GREAT JOB!
THAT WAS AWE-SOME!
UH?!

I'M SO SORRY!
DON'T WORRY. ANYONE BLINDED BY GREED SO EASILY PROBABLY WASN'T THE MAIN CHARACTER TO BEGIN WITH.
OH NOOOO! I'M THE MAIN CHARACTER BUT I WAS TEMPTED BY ALL THIS MONEY! I TOTALLY FORGOT TO HELP OUT!
WAIT IS HE TALKING DOWN ON HIMSELF NOW?
I BELIEVE YOU'RE RIGHT.
I KNEW IT...
LAST NYANMURAI WOULD BE A MUCH BETTER MAIN CHARACTER THAN ME ANYWAY.
HE'S GIVING HIMSELF A PEP TALK?!
YOU'RE STILL A GOOD GUY!
AW, DON'T LET IT GET TO YOU! EVERYONE MAKES A MISTAKE NOW AND AGAIN! ♪
VERY WELL! THIS TIME WE'LL FIGHT TO THE END!
NOT AGAIN ...
ENOUGH! WE'LL DECIDE WHO'S THE MAIN CHARACTER ONCE AND FOR ALL!
ZUFF

CHAPTER 113:

SNAP DECISION YO-KAI DECIDEVIBLE

OSH
SSHH
IT'S SO OBVIOUS.
THIS LOOKS REALLY SERIOUS, RIGHT? BUT IT'LL FIZZLE OUT QUICKLY.

KA-SHA
HE CUT THE LASER BEAM IN TWO!
...
CHKT ...
CHKT ...

CHOOM CHOOM CHOOM CHOOM
HEY... THIS IS GETTING REALLY INTENSE!

SHHHAAAA
COULD... COULD THIS BE...
RIGHT BACK AT YOU.
NOT BAD... I DIDN'T REALIZE YOU WERE THIS GOOD...
AND AFTER THIS THEY BECOME BLOOD-BROTHERS!! WHAT AN EXCITING SCENE!! OOOH!!
B-BMP B-BMP
...A BUDDING FRIENDSHIP?! BIRTHED OUT OF A NEWFOUND RESPECT FOR THEIR RIVAL?!

HAILEY ANNE!
YES, SIR!
WOOOSH
I WILL NEVER RELINQUISH MY TITLE AS MAIN CHARACTER OF THIS MANGA.
OH NO...!
I'M NOT INTERESTED IN BEING THE MAIN CHARACTER ...
...BUT I REFUSE TO BACK DOWN!
OH NO...?
AS AN OUTSIDE OBSERVER ...
...WHICH OF US IS BEST FIT TO BE THE MAIN CHARACTER ?!
WHAT?! HOW CAN I CHOOSE ?!
WELL ...
STRENGTH ISN'T EVERYTHING... A MAIN CHARACTER ALSO NEEDS TO BE LIKABLE...
USAPYON IS... NOT THAT BRIGHT. BUT HIS LOVE FOR DOCTOR HUGHLY IS SO HEARTWARMING!
LAST NYANMURAI IS SO RELIABLE. YOU KNOW THAT YOU CAN ALWAYS COUNT ON HIM!
I...I JUST... I CAN'T DECIDE BETWEEN THE TWO OF YOU!
WHY NOT?! IT SHOULD OBVIOUSLY BE ME!
HELLOOOOO. ♪ I SEE YOU'RE HAVING TROUBLE MAKING A DECISION...
ALLOW ME TO...

...IN THE BLINK OF AN EYE!
VSSH
...MAKE THE DECISION FOR YOU...
!!!
!!!
HMM... WHICH ONE...
...
SHE CAN'T SEE HIM WITHOUT THE WATCH!
HE DID HIS BIG POSE AND SHE'S GOING TO MISS IT!
...
WHAT? A YO-KAI ?!
FWASH
WHOA! WHICH YO-KAI IS THIS?!
AND WHAT'S WITH THAT POSE ?!
WHAT'S HE GOING TO DO? WILL HE REPEAT HIMSELF?
THIS WILL BE INTER-ESTING...

AND MY DECISION IS...I WILL!
NOW I MUST DECIDE ON WHETHER TO INTRODUCE MYSELF AGAIN OR NOT!
HE SURE IS PERSISTENT, HUH?
THAT'S ONE WORD FOR IT...
DON'T WORRY! I'M USED TO PEOPLE BEING STUNNED BY MY PRESENCE!
MAYBE HE SHOULD WORRY SOME...
...
BWAHAHAHA!
DECIDE-VIBLE!
I AM THE INSTAN-TANEOUS, SNAP DECISION YO-KAI...
SNAP DECISION YO-KAI
DECIDEVIBLE
BRRR
Drumroll Please!
AND THE MAIN CHARACTER SHOULD BE...
RRLLLLLL...
YOU'RE STUMPED TRYING TO DE-CIDE WHO SHOULD BE THE MAIN CHARAC-TER, RIGHT ?!
I'LL MAKE THE DECISION FOR YOU! ♪

ME !!
Just kidd--
THAT'S ENOUGH.
SLA ASH

YAAAAOOOW!
HE WAS IRRITATING ME AND FOR SOME REASON ...
...I IMMEDIATELY DECIDED TO ATTACK HIM.
URRGH ...
NICE WORK.
YUP.
BWA HA HA!
EXACTLY! DO YOU SEE?! YOUR SNAP DECISION IS ONLY FURTHER PROOF OF MY INCREDIBLE POWER!
AND NOW IT'S TIME TO SAY FARE-WELL!
WHAT? THAT'S IT? AREN'T YOU GOING TO KEEP FIGHT-ING?!
I'D LOVE TO STAY, HOW-EVER...
...I'VE ALREADY MADE UP MY MIND TO LEAVE!!
?

THE SWORD ATTACK GOT HIM.
...AND BEGONE! ♪
WE'LL FIGHT HIM SOME OTHER TIME.
YEAH...
...

LENGTH (CONTINUED FROM PAGE 29)

CHAPTER 114:
TAKE A BREAK YO-KAI
RE-Q-PERATE

I'M NATE ADAMS.
AN ORDINARY ELEMENTARY SCHOOL STUDENT.
I'M NOT SUPER SMART BUT I'M NOT DUMB EITHER. I'M JUST ORDINARY.
I'M NOT GOOD AT SPORTS OR BAD AT THEM. I'M JUST ORDINARY.
I'M NOT EXCEPTIONALLY POPULAR WITH THE GIRLS AT SCHOOL.
BUT IF THERE'S ONE THING...
I'M HOME.
...THAT'S NOT ORDINARY ABOUT ME...
IT'S WHAT I'M WEARING ...
KRCHK
...ON MY LEFT ARM.
HEY! LET'S GO OUT AND LOOK FOR MORE YO-KAI! ♪
TOSS

FWUMPT

...

COULD IT BE...?!
ALL YOU DID WAS GO TO SCHOOL AND COME BACK HOME--NOTHING SPECIAL, TOTALLY ORDINARY--AND YOU'RE THIS TIRED?!
FWAASH
I KNOW! IT MUST BE A YO-KAI!

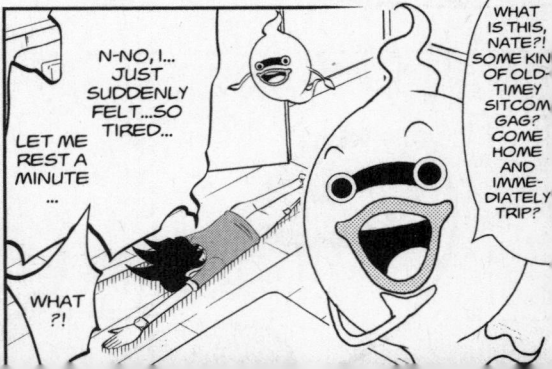
N-NO, I... JUST SUDDENLY FELT...SO TIRED...
LET ME REST A MINUTE ...
WHAT ?!
WHAT IS THIS, NATE?! SOME KIN OF OLD-TIMEY SITCOM GAG? COME HOME AND IMME-DIATELY TRIP?

YO-KAI WHO THINKS HE'S MY BUTLER FOR SOME REASON.
WHAT IS?
THAT'S AMAZING!
NO! YOU'VE BECOME EXCEPTIONALLY WEAK, NATE!
AND THIS IS WHISPER.
YEAH!
OH, A YO-KAI!
YOU'RE NOT ORDINARY ANYMORE! YOU'RE BELOW ORDINARY!

WELL?
AGH!
TWITCH
I'M AWAKE! I'M AWAKE!
HAS HE BEEN ASLEEP ?

THAT MEANS ...
A YO-KAI THAT FORCES TIRED PEOPLE TO GET SOME REST!
THIS IS RE-Q-PERATE!
I FEEL SO BAD FOR YOU!
...THAT YOU'RE STILL TOTALLY ORDINARY, NATE!
HE'S SO AN-NOY-ING ...
NO! A YO-KAI BEING BEHIND THIS MEANS ...
?
I KNOW! HE'S THE REASON THAT I COLLAPSED AS SOON AS I CAME HOME!
SINCE WHEN DO I DO THAT?!
HOW DISRE-SPECTFUL! MY MASTER NATE ADAMS WILL BEAT THE LIVING DAYLIGHTS OUT OF YOU!
QWEEEE
SO HE WAS SLEEP-ING!
HUMPH, COULD YOU STOP SHOUT-ING...?
I JUST WOKE UP!

!!!
FWUUUP

SO I HELPED HIM GET SOME REST.
AGGRESSION AND IRRITABILITY ARE SIGNS THAT YOUR BODY IS TIRED!

IMPOSSIBLE! HOW IS HE UP ALREADY?!

NGHooo

HE'LL BE ASLEEP FOR A WHILE.

IT'S JUST A LUMP!
...
NNGH...
THA-RAT'S RIGHT.
IS IT ALL BECAUSE OF YOU?!
I'M SURE IT'S HAPPENED TO YOU BEFORE!
YOU STRUG-GLE TO GET UP IN THE MORNING ...
YOU DON'T FEEL TIRED BUT YOU PASS OUT ON THE COUCH ...
UGGGH
FATIGUE BUILDS UP INSIDE YOUR BODY EVEN WHEN YOU DON'T REALIZE IT.
THE YO-KAI THAT MAKES YOU LAZY? AND THE ONE THAT MAKES YOU THINK EVERYTHING IS BORING?
YOU FORCE PEOPLE TO LIE DOWN AND SLEEP...YOU'RE KIND OF LIKE CUTTA-NAH AND HORIZON-TAIL!

DON'T YOU DARE COMPARE ME TO THEM!
TAKE A BREAK YO-KAI
RE-Q-PERATE
THEY JUST MAKE PEOPLE LOUNGE AROUND IDLY!
!!!
I HELP PEOPLE REST SO THEY CAN REGAIN THEIR STRENGTH!
HOW ABOUT YOU TELL THEM THAT TO THEIR FACES ?
NO-GOOD SCOUN-DRELS?! HOW COULD YOU SAY THAT?!
THEY'RE JUST TRYING TO LIVE THEIR LIVES TO THE FULLEST TOO!
DON'T TREAT ME LIKE THOSE NO-GOOD SCOUN-DRELS!
I'M IMPOR-TANT! I HELP PEOPLE LIVE THEIR LIVES TO THE FULLEST!

CALLING CUTTA-NAH AND HORIZON-TAIL!
TELL HIM THAT YOU'RE NOT NO-GOOD SCOUN-DRELS!
COME ON, TELL HIM!
YEAH...COULD WE TAKE MORE OF A BREAK BETWEEN SUMMONINGS? A HUNDRED YEARS OR SO?
HNNURRCH
UGH... WHAT IS IT? THIS IS ALREADY SUCH A DRAG.
!!!
WAIT...DID YOU JUST MAKE THEM GO TO SLEEP?!
HAHA...I GUESS I WAS OVER-THINKING THINGS...!
ME TOO.
GOING ALL THE WAY HOME WOULD BE A DRAG, SO I'M GOING TO SLEEP HERE.
OH, I'M... SORRY FOR SUMMON-ING YOU, I GUESS.
REALLY ...?
YEAH, I DON'T REALLY HAVE THE ENERGY TO GET UPSET ABOUT STUFF LIKE THAT.
Call me a scoundrel, whatever...
I DON'T REALLY CARE EITHER WAY. THIS IS A REAL DRAG.

PLIPT
AGH!
I'M AWAKE! I'M AWAKE!
HOW LONG HAVE YOU BEEN ASLEEP ?!
SHFF SHFF
...
DO YOU WANT TO MAKE PEOPLE REST OR DO YOU WANT TO TAKE A NAP? WHICH IS IT?!
HEH HEH HEH, I'M... EXHAUST-ING?
DEALING WITH YOU IS EXHAUST-ING!
JUST GET OUT OF HERE!
YOU FELL BACK ASLEEP THAT QUICKLY?!
TWITCH
AGH!!

AH
HA
YOU'RE CREATING PROBLEMS JUST TO SOLVE THEM!
...I CAN HELP YOU GET SOME REST! ♪
EVERYONE SAYS THAT. BUT DON'T WORRY... ♪
KRRRKT
SO LET'S CALL SOMEONE ELSE! SHOW ME WHAT YOU CAN DO!
BUT HE DOES TEND TO RUN OUT OF BAT-TERIES EASILY...
ROBO-NYAN NEVER GETS TIRED!
ALL RIGHT THEN...I'LL FORCE YOU TO LEAVE!
VOOSH
MEEOOW!
CALLING ...
... TOMNYAN!

YOU NEED TO FIGHT A YO-KAI?
BUT WHY ME?
I THINK YOU'RE JUST THE YO-KAI TO BEAT HIM!
YOU THINK SO MUCH OF ME! WHAT AN HONOR! ♪
...
IF I HELP HIM NOW...
...I CAN CALL IN A FAVOR LATER TO HELP WITH MY TRUE PLANS!
CRYPTIC YO-KAI
TOMNYAN
VOOOSH
LET'S DO IT!
BE CAREFUL! THAT YO-KAI CAN MAKE YOU FALL ASLEEP!
QWEEEE
THE LIGHT! IT'S WHAT KNOCKED WHISPER OUT!

WOOOSH
NOT SO FAST!
FW
UM
P
BUMPT
WHY IS HE IN THE MIDDLE OF THE FLOOR?!
OOKS LIKE I HAVE TO SUMMON ROBONYAN ANYWAY!
...
AW MAN ...
WHOOPS.

I DON'T SEE THEM AS MY ENEMIES. I JUST WANT TO HELP THEM GET SOME REST!
...
HMM... YOU'RE NOT EVEN TRYING TO FINISH THEM OFF, ARE YOU?
WAIT... ARE YOU SLEEP-ING AGAIN?!
AHHH
...

...BUT HE DOESN'T MEAN ANY HARM.
I SEE...I ASSUMED THAT WE WERE GOING TO HAVE TO FIGHT HIM...

THANKS... AND I'M SORRY.

YOU SHOULD GET SOME REST EVERY NOW AND THEN!
YOU'VE ALREADY HELPED SO MANY YO-KAI... MORE THAN ANY OTHER HUMAN!

!!!
SOUNDS LIKE YOU'RE THE ONE WHO NEEDS SOME REST! ♪
...AND YOU KEPT FALLING ASLEEP! YOU MUST BE TIRED AS WELL!
YOU WERE GETTING IRRITATED EARLIER TOO...

NOW I KNOW WHY HE HAS THE YO-KAI WATCH!
REST...NO HUMAN HAS EVER BEEN CONCERNED FOR ME BEFORE...
OKAY!
FSHH
PLEASE GIVE ME A CALL WHENEVER YOU NEED A BREAK!
OKAY, THANKS!
WHY DON'T YOU TAKE A NAP ON MY BED? ♪
I GOT ANOTHER YO-KAI MEDAL! ♪
PO
PT

NATE ADAMS'S CURRENT NUMBER OF YO-KAI FRIENDS: 73

CHAPTER 115:
KLUTZ YO-KAI
CLODZILLA
TAKE THIS! PAWS OF FURY!
FINALLY TODAY, THE DA I BEAT TRUCK
VRRRR
HEY! WATCH OUT! THAT TRUCK'S GOING TO HIT YOU!
CHOW CHOW CHOW
I'VE GOTTA HELP HIM!
DASH
MEOOOOOOOW!
WOOSH
LOOK OOO-OUT!
UFF

THUNCK!
MRRRAO-OWWW!
WHOOPS.
SHUFF
MY ARMS WERE TOO SHORT AND I ACCIDENTALLY HEAD-BUTTED HIM!
KLUTZ YO-KAI
CLODZILLA
WHAT? THERE'S A STRANGE RING AROUND HIS BUTT!
FWOO
NNNGH...
OH...
ARE YOU OKAY? I'M SO SORRY. I'M A KLUTZ YO-KAI AND ALWAYS MESS THINGS UP.
CLOMP CLOMP

HIS ESSENCE IS ESCAPING FROM HIS REAR!
SHOOO
WHAAAAA
NNGH NNGH
GRRN...
I'LL GRAB IT AND PUT IT BACK IN HIS BODY!
SHA
SHA
WHAT SHOULD I DOOO-OOO ?!
SHOOOO

TUNGK!
KRAK
MRRRAAOOOW!
WHA?!
FWEEEE...
TWITCH TWITCH
I'M SORRY! ARE YOU OKAY?
OTHER THAN BE-COMING A GHOST ...
OWWW...

UNNNGH
THE TELE-PHONE POLE!
KA-
THUNK
I MEAN... YOU'RE A YO-KAI...SO YOU'LL BE OKAY... RIGHT?
Heh heh heh...
HUNH?

SHOOO
ANOTHER ONE!
How did his essence end?!
SHU
NKT
I KNOW
SH
UP
I'LL MAKE HIM SWALLOW IT!

IT PASSED RIGHT THROUGH!
SHOOO
WHAAA
ARGH!
MEOW?!
Did the truck beat me again?!
I DON'T WANT TO BE GONE!
SHUFF SHUFF SHUFF
I'LL THROW YOUR BODY UP TO YOU!! GET IN THERE!
TEKI
DO IT FAST!
HERE GOES!
SH
THANK YOU!

AHHH ...!
THU
THAT'S TOO FAST!
PEOPLE WHO ALWAYS MESS THINGS UP MIGHT BE UNDER THE EFFECT OF CLODZILLA!
TWK
BOW
I'M SORRY ...
I WAS ABOUT TO... YOU KNOW!
I BARELY MANAGED IT.
PHEW...

CHAPTER 116: UNINTENTIONAL YO-KAI PUSH PUP

AIYEEEE!
TI
NG
KI
VNNN
WHAAA
UNNNGH
HEY, CAT! WHY DON'T YOU WATCH WHERE YOU'RE WALKING?!
WHAT?
WATCH WHERE I'M DRIVING ...?
WATCH WHERE I'M WALKING? YOU SHOULD WATCH WHERE YOU'RE DRIVING!
I WAS IN THE MIDDLE OF SHOPPING ON MY COMPUTER!
IT WAS TOTALLY OBVIOUS THAT I WASN'T WATCHING THE ROAD!
SO YOU SHOULD HAVE GOTTEN OUT OF THE WAY!
...

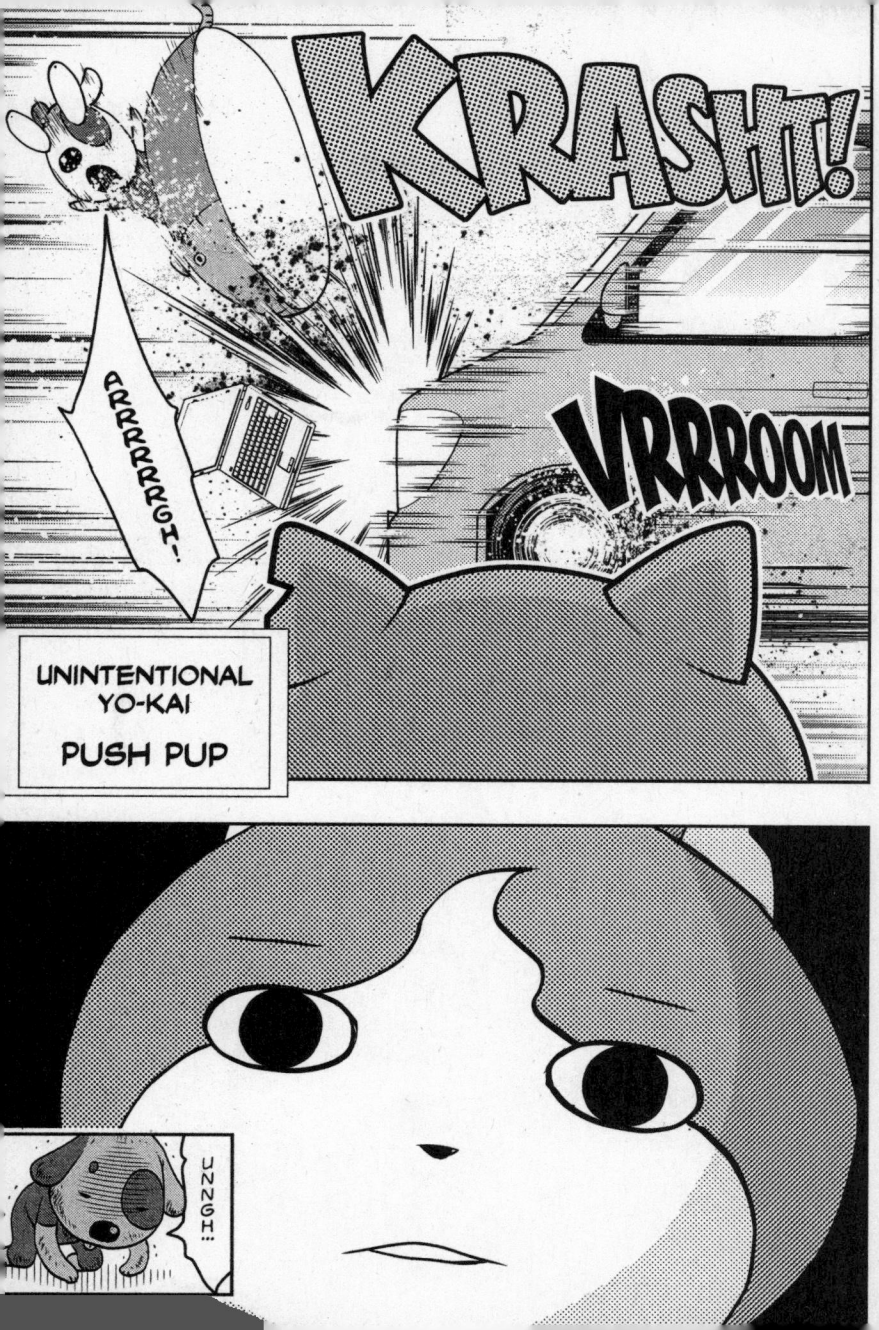
KRASH!!
VRRROOM
ARRRRRRGH!
UNINTENTIONAL YO-KAI
PUSH PUP
UNNGH!!

YOU JUST TOLD ME THE OPPOSITE ...
VROOM
GRRRRR!
HEY! YOU SHOULD WATCH WHERE YOU'RE DRIVING!

KRA-DOOM
ARRRRRGH!
SHUT IT!
THIS IS YOUR FAULT TO BEGIN WITH!
PYU

WHERE... DID YOU EVEN... GET THAT...?!
I FOUND IT. I WASN'T PLANNING ON IT, BUT IT WAS JUST SO EASY!
Too easy...
YOU JUST HAPPENED TO BUY SUCH A THING ?!
I WAS WORRIED THAT IT WAS JUST GOING TO SIT AROUND TAKING UP SPACE FOREVER..
THANKS FOR GIVING ME AN EXCUSE TO USE IT! ♪
WHAAAT?! THERE WAS NO EXCUSE FOR THAT!
DO YOU MIND IF I TAKE THIS OPPOR-TUNITY ...

WHAAAAAAA?
A TANK?! WHAT?! OF COURSE I MIND!
...TO USE THIS TOO ?
KRRCH KRRC
FIRE!
PLIP
NO! STOP-PIT!
I JUST HAP-PENED TO BUY THIS ONLINE AS WELL... ♪
PAWS OF FURY!
CHOW CHOW
CHOW
CHOW
THAT'S IT! I'LL PUNCH THE SHELL BACK AT YOU!

IT SHOOTS LASER BEAMS!
ZIZZ
ZAPT!
WHOA!
BL
AM
VOOOSH
OH, IT FIRES SHELLS TOO!
KA-DOOM!
WHAT?! OF COURSE IT'S DANGER-OUS!
DON'T DODGE IT! IT'S DANGER-OUS!

THOOM
ARRRRRGH!

BE CAREFUL WHAT YOU BUY ON THE INTERNET!
MAYBE YOU SHOULD BUY SOME MEDICINE FIRST...
HRRNNGH
IS THAT EVEN A THING?
I SHOULD HAVE GOT THE TANK... WITH A ROOF ON IT...

CHAPTER 117: ON THE EDGE YO-KAI HUMTEA JUMTEA

HUFF HUFF
I'M REALLY GOING TO DO IT! REALLY!
COME ON ALREADY! HURRY UP!
Just hold on!
TWITCH TWITCH
I'M GONNA DO IT! REALLY I AM!
HUFF
HUFF
SHUDDER
SHUDDER
JUST DO IT!
ARRRRGH!
HUFF HUFF
I'M REALLY, REALLY-- OH.
...
SO I MADE THE RIGHT CHOICE...
HMM?
I...I DIDN'T SAVE HIM. BUT IF I HAD JUST RUSHED IN... WE BOTH WOULD HAVE BEEN HIT.

I HAVE NO OTHER OPTION...I HAVE TO DO IT...I HAVE TO APOLOGIZE SINCERELY!
OH NO! HE'S STILL ALIVE! AND ANGRY! HE'S GOING TO CLOBBER ME!
IT'S GAME OVER!
NNNNNGH
WHY DID YOU EVEN BOTHER GETTING MY HOPES UP?!
FOR STARTERS, JUST COME DOWN HERE!
SHIFF SHIFF
I WAS SO SCARED...I COULDN'T EVEN MOVE!
STOP LOOKING DOWN ON ME, U-GUYZ
SO THIS WAS ALL YOUR FAULT!
YES... I'M SO SORRY!
I'M SORRY! ANYONE I INSPIRIT GETS CONFRONTED WITH A DIRE SITUATION!
ON THE EDGE YO-KAI
HUMTEA JUMTEA
PUP-PUP
HUH?
I KNOW HE'LL CLOBBER ME! BUT AS LONG AS I STAY AWAY, I'LL BE SAFE! I'M GOING HOME–!
I'M NOT GOING DOWN THERE!
EEEEEK!
OH NO! IT'S GAME OVER! I THOUGHT HE'D FORGIVE ME IF I WAS HONEST!

IT'S GAME OVER! HE'S GOING TO PUNCH ME! AND KICK ME! HE'LL KNOCK MY SPIRIT OUT OF MY BODY!
TWANG!
TWANG!
TOO LATE! I CLIMBED UP!
CLIMB CLIMB
...
...
IS THIS YOUR FAULT TOO ?!
FWOOOO
MEOOOOW!
SLLLLIPP!
WHAT ON EARTH ARE YOU BABBLING ABOU--?!
!!!
FWOOO
CLOMPT
HANG ON!
THANKS!
VOOSH!
!
THIS... THIS TIME I'LL SAVE YOU!
BUNGEE JUUUUUMP!
BUNGEE JUMP! A TEST OF COURAGE IN WHICH YOU WRAP A CORD AROUND YOUR LEG AND JUMP FROM A HIGH PLACE.

ARRRRRRGH!
WHOOPS ...
THE ROPE WAS TOO LONG...
CLOUD! UP-UP-UP! QUICKLY!
TUG
TUG
ARE YOU ALL RIGHT?!
...!!!
THIS TIME I...I JUMPED DOWN TO HELP HIM! HE SHOULD FORGIVE ME... RIGHT?
IF YOU HADN'T INTERFERED... I WOULD HAVE BEEN ABLE TO LAND PROPERLY!
NOW HE'S MAD!
IT'S GAME OVER!

WHAT ...?!
ALL THE TROUBLE YOU'VE CAUSED ME...I FORGIVE YOU.
BUT THANKS FOR AT LEAST TRYING TO HELP!

I THOUGHT IT WAS GAME OVER...BUT I MUSTERED ALL MY COURAGE! ♪
I MADE IT THROUGH... THIS HORRIBLE SITUATION...!

VRROOM
...
THUNGK
ARRRRRGH!

SHIF SHIF
URGH ...
ARE YOU OKAY ?

SWINGING

WHAT IS HE BLAMING ME FOR?!
THIS IS ALL BECAUSE I INSPIRITED YOU!
HUFF HUFF
YOU'RE SUCH A NUISANCE!
VOOOOSH
I'M GONNA CLOBBER YOU!
YAAAAAAAAAH!
ARE YOU KIDDING ME?! YOU'LL REGRET THIS!
SHUMP

WHOOPS ...
...
SPROOOING
ARRRGH!! CLOUD! COME DOWN! DOWN, I SAID! DOWN!
MMMMNGH...
AHHHH!
P-TOIIIING
ARRRRRRGH!
I'M GOING HOME.
THU
NGKT
VRRO

CHAPTER 118:
BATH LOVER YO-KAI
LIL BLUE BATHING HOOD

SHWAAA
WHAAAAAT?!
YOU'RE TAKING A BATH IN THE MIDDLE OF THE STREET?!
AND NOT ONLY THAT... THEY ALSO THINK I'M WEIRD FOR WEARING A HOOD IN THE BATH! THEY WON'T EVEN LOOK AT ME!
WHAAAAAT?! USUALLY PEOPLE THINK I'M WEIRD FOR BATHING IN PUBLIC! THEY JUST STOP AND STARE!
RRRMM
BBLLEEE
YEAH! YEAH! YEAH! YEAH!
IT'S MY LUCKY DAY! ♪ MAKE SOME ROOM! I'M COMING IN! ♪
WOOHOO! ♪

HE'S ALREADY GOTTEN IN AND COMFORT-ABLE!
WHAAA?!
AHHHHHHHHHH
IS THAT SO...?

I KNOW... BUT I JUST COULDN'T HELP MYSELF!
YOU'RE SUPPOSED TO RINSE YOURSELF BEFORE GETTING IN A PUBLIC BATH!

I AM A O-KAI THAT SOOTHES PEOPLE BY GIVING THEM THE PERFECT BATHING EXPERI-ENCE!
TEMPERA-TURE, WATER PURITY, WATER HARDNESS, THE AMOUNT OF WATER... EVERYTHING ABOUT THIS BATH IS PERFECT. ♪

SCRUB
SCRUB
SO YOU NOTICED!
IT FEELS SOOOOOO GOOD. ♪

SHUPT
NOT A BIT! LOOK...

THE TUB IS PART OF YOU?!
YOU MUST BE EXAGGER-ATING!
WHAT?! ARE YOU SERIOUS?!
BATH LOVER YO-KAI
LIL BLUE BATHING HOOD
I LOVE BATHS SO MUCH THAT THIS TUB IS ACTUALLY PART OF ME! ♪

...
HAHA!
MY LEGS ARE DOWN HERE... AND UP THERE!
I EVOLVED AN EXTRA PAIR! ♪
...
SPLOOOOO
AGGGGH! WHEN I STOOD UP, ALL THE WATER POURED OUT!

WAIT...IF YOU AND THE TUB ARE FUSED TOGETHER.. WHERE DOES THE WATER COME FROM?
OH, THIS?
SHWAAA
I HAVE TO FILL IT BACK UP!
YOU MEAN YOU'RE TAKING A BATH IN YOUR PEE?!
WHAAAAA
HAHAHA♪
IT'S ALL THE WATER AND OTHER DRINKS THAT I'VE HAD IN THE PAST DAY OR SO! ♪
HAAAAA
HE'S... HE'S RIGHT!
...
...

AHHH! IT'S HOT!
SHWAAA
IT'S HOT, DIRTY PEE!
IT IS NOT!
SWIPT
NO! NO NO NO NO! IT'S NOT! IT'S NOT PEE! IT'S NOT!
?
BUT THANKS TO YOU...
SIZZLE SIZZLE
HEH HEH HEH. ♪ WHEN I GET MAD, THE WATER TEMPERATURE RISES. ♪

I'M NOT GETTING IN YOUR HOT PEE BATH!
AHHHHHH
NOW THE TUB IS NICE AND STEAMY! ♪
Climb on in! ♪

PLIP-PLIP
OH...

AGGGGGGH!
SHWW
IT'S NOT PEE!

THE STOPPER ...?
I AL-READY TOLD YOU...
POP

OF COURSE YOU ARE! YOU CAN'T JUST KEEP PEEING FOREVER!
HMMM
AWW
I'M ALL OUT OF WATER...

AGGGGH, IT'S HOT! AND IT'S COMING OUT OF HER BUTT! GROSS!
FWOOOH
IT'S NOT PEE! DRAINAGE ATTACK!
NO, IT'S NOT!
...BUT NOW I NEED ANOTHER BATH TO WASH AWAY THE PEE!
NNNGH
MY SWEAT GOT WASHED AWAY...
HUFF HUFF
SO RUDE
TMP TMP

CHAPTER 119: UNPREDICTABLE YO-KAI UNBELIEVABOY!

HAHAHA
WALKING AROUND NAKED IN THE COLD?! YOU'RE THE ONE WHO'S WEIRD!
YOU'RE SO WEIRD...IT'S UNBELIEV-ABLE!
UNBELIEVABLE!
YOU'RE GOING TO CATCH A COLD...
BUCK NAKED IN THE MIDDLE OF WINTER! ARE YOU SURPRISED? PRETTY UNBELIEVABLE, HUH?
TA-DAAH!
A YO-KAI THAT LOVES SURPRISING PEOPLE BY DOING THE UNEX-PECTED!
I'M UNBELIEV-ABOY!!!
BUT...
OH, I'LL BE FINE. ♪
UNPREDICTABLE YO-KAI
UNBELIEVABOY!
He usually wears a diaper.

SHIVERS CHILLS SHUDDER
THAT'S TOTALLY A COLD.
Am I imagining this?
...FOR SOME REASON, I SUDDENLY GOT A CHILL, MY THROAT HURTS AND I CAN'T STOP SHIVERING...

YOU'RE DOING EXACTLY WHAT PEOPLE WITH COLDS DO!
REALLY?! THAT'S UNBELIEVABLE!
KOFF KOFF
BEEP
ICE
OH COME ON! IT CAN'T BE THAT! IMPOSSIBLE!

HA HA HA.
YOUR CAPE! THAT MUST BE HOW YOU FLY!
AH-HA!
FWOOM

ARE YOU SURPRISED? PRETTY UNBELIEVABLE, HUH?
WHAT? THAT CAME OUT OF NOWHERE ...
I CAN FLY, YOU KNOW!
ANYWAY, LET'S CHANGE THE SUBJECT ...

I can't survive without it.

SHUDDER

SHUDDER

SHUDDER

THIS? THIS IS TO PROTECT ME FROM THE COLD!

SO HE IS COLD AFTER ALL!

TREMBLE

TREMBLE

PUT SOMETHING ELSE ON!

POOOOF
YAH!
HE FARTS ?!
UGGGH
P-P-POOF
ARE YOU SURPRISED? TOTALLY UNBELIEVABLE, ISN'T IT?!
PRETTY AMAZING, RIGHT? ♪
...
POOF
POOF
POOF
POOF POOF POOF
I CAN FLY AS SLOW OR FAST AS I WANT JUST BY ADJUSTING MY FARTS. ♪
UNBELIEVABLE, RIGHT?
IT'S... PRETTY IMPRESSIVE ...
...BUT NOTHING TO BE PROUD OF. OR BRAG ABOUT. OR SHOW TO PEOPLE.
OH NO ...

WHAAAT?!
FWOOOO
POOF
IF I CAN'T FART...I FALL!
VOOOM
LOOK OUT!
VRRRRRR
MEOW?! IT'S A TRUCK!

ULPT...

BURPS MAKE YOU FLY TOO?!
BURPPP
WHY MEEEEEE ?!
THUN
GKT
UNBELIEVABLE...!
...
HRRNGH
TWITCH TWITCH
TWITCH TWITCH
UNBELIEVABLE!
I CAN'T BELIEVE YOU JUMPED OUT IN FRONT OF THAT TRUCK...

CHAPTER 120:
HERBIVORE YO-KAI
HERBIBOY
INSTEAD, I THINK I'LL THANK THE CARS FOR GIVING ME SO MUCH ENTERTAIN-MENT.
AH, THERE IT IS NOW.
I'VE BEEN FIGHTING TRUCKS FOR SO LONG... BUT NOW IT'S TIME TO STOP.
VRROOM...
I DON'T... GET IT...
HNNGH
TWITCH
TWITCH...
ARRRRRRRGH!
TH
UNGK
MR. TRUCK, THANK YOU FOR--

I KNOW...!
THERE MUST BE A YO-KAI AROUND!
I DON'T FEEL LIKE FIGHTING OR DOING ANYTHING!
MUNCH MUNCH
HEH HEH HEH ...
THUNGK
EVERYTHING'S GOING DARK...I'LL JUST... GIVE UP...
NOT THAT I REALLY CARE...
SHUPT...
WHAT ?!
YEEAAH!
I HAVE TO BE REUNITED WITH AMY!
WHAT?! NO! NO, I'M GOING TO LIVE!

YOU'RE GOING TO KEEP LIVING ?!
SERIOUSLY?!
?
ULPT!
URRGH
KOFF KOFF
YOU SHOCKED ME SO MUCH THAT I GOT GRASS STUCK IN MY THROAT!
GRASS ?!
TUMP TUMP
FWUMP
KOFF...
OH FORGET IT. I'LL JUST GIVE UP.
WHAAAAT?!
SHUP
HMM... I SURVIVED...
E'S STILL EATING GRASS?!

MUNCH MUNCH
I'M A HERBIVORE YO-KAI THAT AVOIDS COMPETITION AND CONFLICT.
I PREFER TO LIVE A LIFE OF UTTER PEACE AND QUIET.
HERBIVORE YO-KAI
HERBIBOY
WHAT?
WHAT A PLAIN, BORING ABILITY! GET OUT OF HERE! WHO NEEDS YA?!
MEEOOW!
BUT THAT'S SO DULL!
WAIT...YOU'RE ENGAGING IN CONFLICT! WHAT ABOUT YOUR BIG INTRODUCTION?!
I LIKE IT HERE AND DON'T WANT TO MOVE!
YOU GO AWAY!

THIS PLACE HAS EXCELLENT GRASS! ♪
AHA! YOU WANT THE GRASS FOR YOURSELF!
OF COURSE I DON'T. JUST LEAVE ALREADY...
WHAAAAA
OR ELSE I'LL HAVE TO FORCE YOU!
KRRK KRRK
I HATE FIGHTING, BUT I WON'T JUST LET YOU BEAT ME UP...
HMM...SO YOU'RE ACCEPTING THE CHALLENGE? INTERESTING ...
OKAY THEN ...

PAWS OF FURY!
VIO-LENCE ISN'T THE ANSWER!
GIVE PEACE A CHANCE!
SAFETY FIRST!
STAY IN SCHOOL!
WHAT?! YOU'RE JUST GOING TO SHOUT SLOGANS AT ME?!

HRRNNGH
THAT WAS SO EASY...

I AVOID FIGHTS BECAUSE OF HOW WEAK I AM...
BUT IF YOU GIVE IT YOUR ALL, YOU'LL NEVER HAVE REGRETS, EVEN IF YOU LOSE!

MAYBE YOU'RE RIGHT. I'LL TRY TO BE MORE LIKE YOU AND GIVE IT MY ALL!
MUNCH MUNCH
CHOMP CHOMP
I HAVE TO KEEP EATING GRASS FOR ENERGY! ♪
THAT'S THE SPIRIT! ♪
OH.
?

NOT AGAIN!
COUGH COUGH
URRRRGH.
URRGH! IT'S STUCK IN MY THROAT!
TUMP TUMP
I... GUESS THAT COUNTS AS MOTIVATION?
THE AFTER-LIFE WAS SO FAR AWAY... SO I DECIDED NOT TO BOTHER GOING.
I'LL MAKE AN EFFORT TO TRY AND DO MY BEST.
SWIP
SH W
OH? HE'S COMING BACK!
FISH
WHAT?! JUST WHEN YOU WERE GOING TO GIVE IT YOUR ALL!
UNNNH

CHAPTER 121: LISTENING YO-KAI NAANDHI

FISH
END OF THE YEAR / NEW YEAR'S SHOP OPENING SCHEDULE
HMM, IS THAT SO?
TELL ME WHAT'S TROUBLING YOU.

FISH
TELL ME WHAT'S

FISH

THAT'S RIGHT. I'M A LISTEN-ING YO-KAI
LISTENING YO-KAII
NAANDHI
WAIT... THAT'S IT?! YOU JUST LISTEN?!

WE'RE SUPPOSED TO BE LIKE, "OH, IT WAS BECAUSE OF A YO-KAI" WHEN SOMETHING HAPPENS! THAT'S HOW THIS WORKS!
YO-KAI ARE SUPPOSED TO DO SOMETHING WHEN THEY INSPIRIT SOMEONE!
WHAAAAA
ARR-RRGH!
IS THAT SO?
YEAH, YEAH, I KNOW! YOU'RE JUST GONNA SAY, "IS THAT SO?" AGAIN, RIGHT?
...
I'D PUNCH YOU IF YOU WEREN'T AN OLD MAN!

SWAAAAPT
HUURGH!
YOU FOOL!
AS LONG AS YOU KEEP RELYING ON VIOLENCE TO SOLVE YOUR PROBLEMS ...
...YOU'LL NEVER ACHIEVE YOUR GOAL!
WHY'S HE SCOLDING ME ALL OF A SUDDEN ?!
HEY! HOW CAN YOU TELL ME NOT TO USE VIOLENCE AFTER YOU JUST ATTACKED ME?!

BAAAAM
ARE YOU SERIOUS ?
LIKE I'M GOING TO FALL FOR THAT!
I DIDN'T USE VIOLENCE. I JUST SMACKED YOU WITH A NAAN! ♪
SWAPT
SWAPT
WHAT?! ARE YOU MOCKING ME?!
THIS IS VIO-LENCE!
I WAS HOLDING BACK BECAUSE YOU'RE AN OLD MAN, BUT I'VE HAD ENOUGH OF THIS!
NAAN IS A TYPE OF INDIAN BREAD EATEN WITH CURRY.
SWAPT
SWAPT
HA HA HA ...

I MAY LOOK OLD, BUT I'M ACTUALLY ONLY 17...
HA HA HA...
YOU'RE SO YOUNG!
WHAAAA
JUST KIDDING! ♪ I'M NOT ACTUALLY. ♪
...
HEY! THIS IS YOUR CHANCE TO SAY IT! TO GO, "IS THAT SO?" WHY AREN'T YOU SAYING IT?!
WHAA?!
THAT'S IT...
...I'M GOING TO CLOBBER YOU!
CHOOM
CHOOM
CHOOM
CHOOM
GRRR!

THOOM
THOOM
THOOM
I'M SORRY I WENT TOO FAR.
I FEEL AWFUL!
NNNG
GASP... GASP...
IT'S OKAY... DON'T WORRY ABOUT IT...
OH NO, HE'S SO OLD...I REALLY OVERDID IT!
NNGH
twitch
twitch
YOU'RE... STRONGER THAN I THOUGHT...
LOOK! A TRUCK! I'LL CHALLENGE IT!
VRROOM
YOU HAVE TO STAY CALM!
MEOW!
NO... YOU JUST BEAT ME UP REALLY BAD.
Urgh...
I SEE! DID YOU... DID YOU LOSE ON PURPOSE JUST TO TEACH ME THAT LESSON?
...YOU'LL ALSO LOSE THE FIGHT!
!!!
OVER-DOING IT MEANS YOU LOST YOUR COOL...
...AND IF YOU LOSE YOUR COOL IN BATTLE...

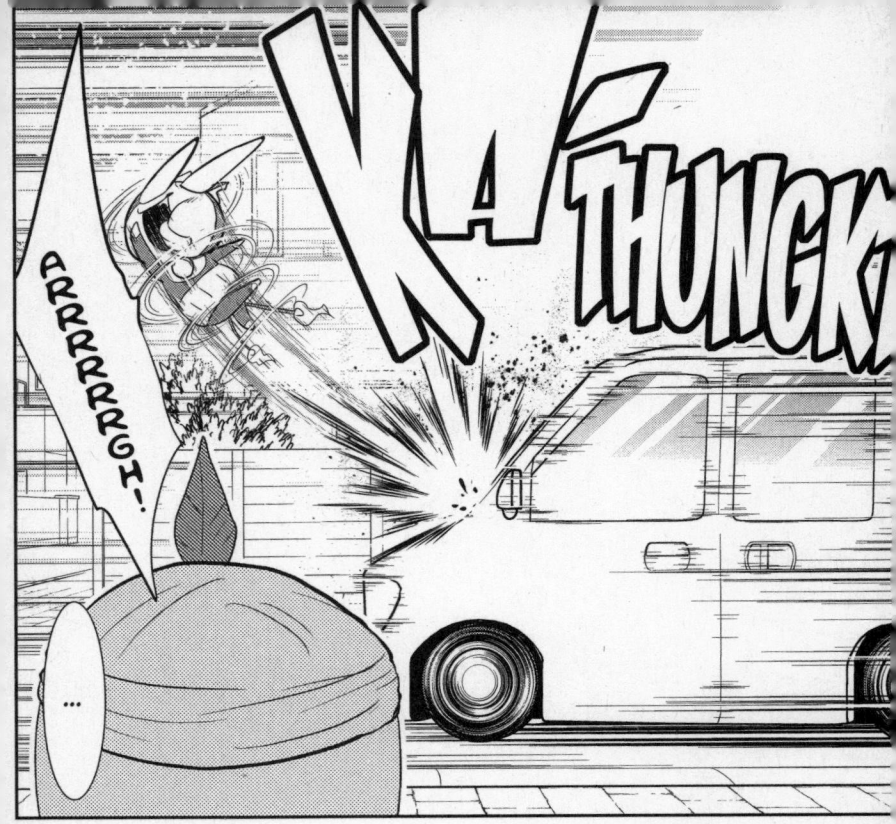
KA-THUNGK
ARRRRRRGH!
...

IS...IS THAT SO...?
YOU JUST DON'T HAVE WHAT IT TAKES.
HE AT'S TROUBLIN YOU.

CHAPTER 122: WITCH GIRL YO-KAI MAGINYAN

FIRE! GO!
FOOOOSH!
AHHH!
FWOOOSH
ARR-RRRGH! DON'T SHOOT IT AT ME!
OH NO! SORRY!
SOME-TIMES MY AIM IS OFF!
PFFFT
IT'S NOT A LAUGHING MATTER!
YOU'RE RIGHT! HA HA! ♪
...
SIZZLE SIZZLE...
THEN YOU SHOULDN'T BE THROW-ING FIRE AROUND!

YOU'RE A... WITCH?!
LIKE THE MONSTERS THAT CURSE PEOPLE AND GIVE THEM POISONED APPLES?!
MY NAME IS MAGINYAN. ♪
Nice to meet you. ♪
WITCH GIRL YO-KAI
MAGINYAN
OKAY, NO PROBLEM! ♪
I JUST WANT TO BAKE THIS SWEET POTATO...
NO THANK YOU.
WOULD YOU LIKE IT?
THAT'S RIGHT! ♪ I'VE EVEN GOT AN APPLE RIGHT HERE! ♪
FSSH
FIRE! GO!
IF YOU'RE WORRIED, JUST GET OUT OF THE WAY! ♪
OKAY ...
PLEASE AIM CAREFULLY...
FOOOO
ONE MORE TRY!

I CAN'T DODGE THAT!
FWOOOOSH!
IT'S BEEN BURNT TO ASHES...
INGI...
...THE SWEET POTATO IS BAKED, RIGHT?
HA HA. WELL ...
SIZZLE SIZZLE...
WHY DID YOU MAKE SO MUCH? IT WAS LIKE A SOUL-TIMATE MOVE!

FIRE IS TOO DANGER-OUS TO MAKE MISTAKES WITH!
JUST KNOCK IT OFF!
ALL YOU DO IS COMPLAIN!
EVERYONE MAKES MISTAKES, YOU KNOW!
HEY... YOU'RE SCARING ME!
FWOOM
GRRRRRR! I'LL BURN YOU TO ASHES! EAT FLAME!
ARRRRRRGH!
FWOOOM
FIRE! GO!

FWOOOSH
WHAT?! NO!
THE FIRE'S ATTACKING HER?! SHE'S TERRIBLE AT THIS...
YOU'RE UNBELIEVABLE... WATER! WE NEED WATER!
HOT! HOT!
I KNOW! I'LL PUT IT OUT WITH MAGIC!
FWOOOOM
BLIZZARD GO!
OOOO! THAT'S A GREAT IDEA! ♪

I...WAS GOING TO ASK...THE SAME... THING...
KRRRRK
WHAAAAT?! WHY DID IT FREEZE YOU?!
GET IT! USE THE ICE TO PUT OUT THE FIRE!
FWOO FWOO
SIZZLE SIZZLE
I KNOW! GRAB AHOLD OF ME!
EXACTLY!♪
FSSSSSSH
GLOMP
AND USE THE FIRE TO MELT THE ICE! A TWO-FOR-ONE DEAL! ♪

AIYEEEEE!
URRGH! WHY COULDN'T YOU BE MORE CAREFUL?!
KRRRKT
HNNGH
THEY FIGURED IT OUT AFTER A FEW DAYS...
PLEASE... DON'T TRY TO FIX IT...
HMM... A SPELL THAT PUTS BROKEN THINGS BACK TO-GETHER ...

CHAPTER 123: NO-GOOD YO-KAI NUMMSKULL

NOW I'M IN THE MIDDLE OF THE FOREST!
SHFF
EEEEEEEE!
HOW DO I KEEP GETTING LOST?! WHERE AM I?!
WHAAAAAT?!
...
VERY IMPRESSIVE! I'VE NEVER SEEN SOMEONE BECOME THIS MUCH OF A STUMBLEBUM!
SWIP
?
OH! THERE YOU ARE!
!!!
SHF
SHF

IN OTHER WORDS, THEY BECOME KLUTZES! AWKWARD FOOLS! TOTALLY INEPT!
MY NAME IS NUMMSKULL !!
PEOPLE I INSPIRIT BECOME HOPELESS STUMBLE-BUMS!
NO-GOOD YO-KAI NUMMSKULL
IT'S ONE THING TO CALL MYSELF THAT, BUT I CAN'T STAND OTHER PEOPLE SAYING IT!
WHAAAAAT?!
YOU CAN'T EVEN KEEP TRACK OF WHO YOU'RE TALKING TO... YOU'RE THE KLUTZ!
SWIP
OH, YOU'RE OVER THERE.
...
WHY ...?!
SO ANNOYING.
WHY ARE YOU DOING ALL THIS?!
BAAAM
I'M OVER HERE ...
APOLOGIZE TO ME
SO ...
RMBBLEE
HEH HEH HEH... I DON'T WANT TO BE THE ONLY STUMBLEBUM.

...I'M GOING TO DRAG EVERY-ONE DOWN WITH ME!
SPLUB...
THUNGK
...
UGGGH!
ARRRGH! I STEPPED IN POOP!
Filthy animals!
BOING
FWUMPT
ARE YOU A KLUTZ OR JUST REALLY UNLUCKY?

YOU FELL RIGHT BACK INTO THE POOP YOU STEPPED IN!
You just can't win!
SP LU UB...
EWWW ...
Something smells...
LATER.
SURE. IF THAT'S WHAT YOU THINK, THEN JUST STOP INSPIRITING ME.
SHFF SHFF
YOU MUST BE A BAD LUCK YO-KAI!
THIS IS ALL BECAUSE I INSPIRITED YOU!
NO ...
ARE YOU UPSET ABOUT HOW CLUMSY YOU ARE?
SOB SOB...
OWW ...
DID YOU STEP IN POOP AGAIN?
SHFF
WHAT IS IT THIS TIME?
WAAAUUUGH!

WELL... THIS IS A FIRST.
NNG... NNG
THE POOP IS STING-ING MY EYES!
SHWAAAA
TUG
NNG NNG
ZLLLSSH
FOR CRYING OUT LOUD... COME WITH ME!
I'M SURE YOU'RE HAVING A ROUGH TIME, BUT... HUH?
I'VE MET PLENTY OF YO-KAI WHOSE POWERS CAUSE THEM TROUBLE...
A FRIEND OF MINE ONCE SAID... ♪
YOU SEE ...
THAT'S OKAY.
I'M SORRY THAT I CAUSED YOU SO MUCH TROUBLE.
THANK YOU... I'M BETTER NOW...
SPLISH SPLOSH

ZZZ...
GRRRRRR!
HE'S NOT EVEN LISTENING!
WHAT?! WHY ARE YOU PUNCHING ME?!
PAWS OF FURY!
YOU'RE GOING TO SELF-DESTRUCT?! ARE YOU NUTS?! STOP IT!
NUMMSKULL DEMISE IS NUMMSKULL'S SOULTIMATE MOVE IN WHICH HE SELF-DESTRUCTS, TURNING EVERYONE AROUND HIM INTO A KLUTZ!
SOULTIMATE MOVE, NUMMSKULL DEMISE!
KSSSHHH
GRRR! I'LL TURN YOU INTO A TOTAL, COMPLETELY IRREDEEMABLE KLUTZ!
SPLOOSH
AHHH!
I REFUSE!

THE RIVER IS CARRYING HIM AWAY...
It was all... pointless.
KRA-DOOM
EAT THIS!
SHWAAAA
...
SHWAAA
SHWAAAA
IF EVERYTHING KEEPS GOING WRONG FOR YOU, YOU MIGHT BE INSPIRED BY HUMMSKULL!
HUH...? WHAT WAS HIS NAME AGAIN ...?
NO... I'LL NEVER... NEVER FOR-GIVE HIM! THAT...
PLIP
HUNH
WHAT A KLUTZ...

CHAPTER 124: KICKBACK YO-KAI ULTERIA

OOO! I CAN COPY IT?! THANKS, BEAR!
HERE, NATE. USE THIS.
MATH
IT'S TOO LATE TO DO ANYTHING ABOUT IT. YOU'RE GOING TO GET IN TROUBLE.
ARRRGGH!
I COMPLETELY FORGOT TO DO MY HOMEWORK!
RRMMBLEE
NO PROBLEM.

NATE! THIS IS NOT OKAY!
HOMEWORK ISN'T JUST BUSYWORK-- IT HELPS YOU LEARN BY REVIEWING WHAT WAS COVERED IN CLASS AND GETTING YOU READY FOR THE NEXT DAY!
COPYING SOMEONE ELSE'S HOMEWORK MIGHT SAVE YOU TIME NOW, BUT IT'S ONLY GOING TO HURT YOU IN THE LONG RUN!
IF YOU REALLY THINK ABOUT IT, COPYING IS JUST A WASTE OF TIME, AS YOU'LL LEARN NEITHER THE MATERIAL IN THE LESSON NOR THE IMPORTANCE OF ACTUALLY DOING YOUR HOMEWORK! UNDER-STAND?
WHISPER.
SO YOU GET IT?
WHAAAAAA
GET OUT OF THE WAY. YOU'RE BLOCKING THE NOTE-BOOK.
DING DONG DING
BYE-BYE. ♪
HA HA HA HA
BYE!
WHISPER... I WAS WRONG...

AHH... THIS IS REALLY GREAT! ♪
Thanks so much for returning the favor! ♪
URGH...I DIDN'T REALIZE... HE WAS GOING TO ORDER ME AROUND... TO REPAY HIM...
I SHOULD HAVE... DONE MY HOME-WORK...
THAT'S GOOD TO HEAR, NATE!
BUT SINCE IT WAS ME THAT HELPED YOU LEARN THAT LESSON...
...YOU CAN CARRY ME ANOTHER 300 FEET TO THANK ME!
NO WAY!
WHAT ?!
WHAAAAT?!
I TAUGHT YOU THE IMPORTANCE OF DOING YOUR HOMEWORK AND YOU'RE NOT EVEN GOING TO THANK ME?!
GRRRRRR
WHY ARE YOU BEING SO CONDE-SCEND-ING?!
COULD IT BE...
FWAAASH

WELL, ACTUALLY...
THERE'S NO SUCH YO-KAI, NATE...
MAYBE IT'S A... CAULDRON-CENDING YO-KAI OR SOME-THING?!
HMM... ALL I SEE...
FSH!
HA HA. ♪
AHH
SO THERE IS A YO-KAI AFTER ALL! WHY DIDN'T YOU SAY SO?!
...IS THIS MYSTERI-OUS YO-KAI OVER HERE!

TA-DAAH
IT'S THE YO-KAI ULTERIA!
KICK-BACKS?
A YO-KAI THAT ASKS FOR KICKBACKS EVERY TIME SHE DOES SOMETHING!
KICKBACK YO-KAI
ULTERIA
SHA
WOW... THAT WAS EASY...
SURE!
HEY! GET AWAY FROM BEAR!
NO WONDER BEAR'S ACTING LIKE THIS!
IN OTHER WORDS... SHE WANTS TO BE REPAID.
HUNH
WHAT?
Why?
SEE WHAT I'M TALKING ABOUT?
OKAY! I DID JUST LIKE YOU SAID... ♪
...NOW GIMME SOME-THING! ♪

IT SERVES HIM RIGHT FOR ORDERING ME AROUND.
NATE... AREN'T YOU GOING TO HELP BEAR?
YOU'RE ABSOLUTELY TERRIBLE! YOU'RE JUST GOING TO USE AND ABANDON ME LIKE THIS?!
YOU MONSTER! HOW COULD YOU?!
OKAY...KEEP INSPIRITING HIM THEN.
IT'S JUST GOING TO RUIN BEAR'S REPUTATION. IT'S NOT MY PROBLEM.
WHAT DO YOU MEAN? ARE YOU JUST BABBLING TO YOURSELF OR WHAT?
...
AGGGGH!
OH NOOOO! I WAS TALKING TO A YO-KAI IN FRONT OF SOMEONE WHO CAN'T SEE THEM! AND EVEN WORSE...I WAS TALKING BAD ABOUT HIM!
A... YO-KAI ...? YOU BRING THEM UP KINDA FREQUENTLY ...
UHM...
I GET IT NOW! NATE ...
HMMM

I'M GLAD HE'S SLOW TO CATCH ON...
REIN IT IN, MAN.
...YOU MUST LIVE IN SOME KINDA FANTASY WORLD. THAT'S WHY YOU FORGOT YOUR HOME-WORK.
Later.

...
WHY AREN'T YOU FOLLOW-ING HIM?

...

STOP BAD-MOUTHING ME!
LISTEN UP, EVERYONE! THIS GUY IS SO CHEAP AND STINGY! YOU WON'T EVEN BELIEVE IT!
WAH! WAH!
OH...

WAUGH! SOMEONE, PLEASE! THIS MAN HAS DECEIVED ME!
...
I DON'T BELIEVE THIS! NOW YOU'RE TRYING TO GET RID OF ME, STILL WITHOUT GIVING ME ANYTHING IN RETURN!

KRRRKT
YO-KAI MEDAL, DO YOUR THING!
CALLING ...
AHHH
I'VE HAD ENOUGH! I'M GOING TO TEACH YOU A LESSON!
...SO YOU ARE GOING TO GIVE ME SOMETHING THEN!
THIS ISN'T JUST ASKING FOR KICKBACKS... YOU'RE BLACK-MAILING ME!
... LAST NYAN-MURAI!
VRRRRRN
I SEE! NYANMURAI ACTS SELF-LESSLY AND RESPECT-FULLY! YOU'RE GOING TO TEACH HER HOW TO DO THE SAME!

KA-THNK

WHAT HAPPENED?

WHY IS IT JUST YOUR HEAD?!
URRGH ...!
SQUEEEE
LET GO! LET ME GO!
HEY! STOP-PIT!
WAIT...IS THERE SOME-ONE ELSE THERE ?!
MEEOOW!
GRRRR
HE'S GETTING SUCKED BACK IN! THIS HAS NEVER HAPPENED BEFORE!
...
HE'S COMING BACK OUT!

MEEEOOOW!
TOMNYAN?!
WHAT?! I DIDN'T CALL FOR YOU!
YEAH, I KNOW! YOU NEVER CALL ME! SO I KEPT AN EYE ON JIBANYAN SINCE YOU CALL HIM ALL THE TIME...
...I WAS JUST WAITING FOR MY OPPOR-TUNITY!
EVER SINCE I DEBUTED, I HAVEN'T HAD MUCH TO DO IN THE MANGA. AND ON TOP OF THAT...

...SOMETIMES I DON'T APPEAR IN A SINGLE PANEL! WHAT KIND OF TREATMENT IS THAT?!
...I SHOULD BE A MAIN CHARACTER IN EVERY CHAPTER!
HUFF HUFF HUFF
YOU NEED TO APOLOGIZE TO ALL OF THE TOMNYAN FANS AROUND THE WORLD FOR HOW YOU'VE TREATED ME!
DON'T WORRY, TOMNYAN!
WOULD YOU KNOCK IT OFF!? THIS ISN'T ABOUT YOU!!
YEAH! ME TOO! LOOK, I'M ON THE COVER OF THE VERY FIRST VOLUME! ♪
YO-KAI WATCH!
THEN ...
WHAAAAAAAT?!
MEEOOW!
NO ONE'S COMPLAINED!
I DON'T THINK ANY OF OUR READERS HAVE MISSED YOU AT ALL! ♪
Seriously!

AWWWW
YOU'RE SULKING ...?
...JUST FORGET ABOUT IT.

OH REALLY ...
YEEAAH!
NO WAY. HE WAS THRILLED FOR A DAY OFF!
YOU MEAN... BY FORCE ?!
GUMP!
I CON-VINCED HIM TO GIVE ME THE LEADING ROLE BEFORE I CAME OUT...
HMPH
AND JIBANYAN ISN'T COMING OUT...?

WHAT?
LEAVE IT TO ME! ♪ I'LL MAKE THIS MANGA EXCITING AGAIN! ♪
NOW NOW ...
HMPH!
BUT I DON'T EVEN CARE WHAT HAPPENS IN THIS MANGA ANYMORE.

B-BAAM
JUST GIMME SOMETHING IN RETURN!
THAT'S ENOUGH! JUST GET OUT OF HERE!
OKAY, I'LL LEAVE ...
...IF YOU GIMME SOMETHING.
AGGGH, SHE'S SO ANNOYING!
TOMNYAN! COULD YOU CHASE HER AWAY?!
!
PLEASE!
AHA! FINALLY! AN OPPORTUNITY FOR ME TO SHINE!
VSH
I'LL BECOME THE MAIN CHARACTER BY DRIVING HER AWAY IN AN IMPRESSIVE FASHION!
!!!
CENTI ...
VO
VSH

EEEEEK!!!
CHOOM
CHOOM
CHOOM
CHOOM
CHOOM
...
CUFFS!
WHAAAAAT?!
WHAT?
SHUPT
I'LL GIVE YOU SOME-THING IF YOU HELP ME!

OOOF! AGGGH! URGH!
WHISPEEEER!
THUD
THUD
THANK YOU FOR SAVING ME...
Are you okay?
TWITCH-TWITCH...
I...I NEVER MEANT... TO HELP YOU...
OH...THEN I GUESS I DON'T HAVE TO THANK YOU! ♪
AN APOLOGY... WOULD BE NICE THOUGH...
GRRRR
!!!
VOOSH
LET'S TRY THIS AGAIN!

SHUT
STOP IT!
WHAT?! YOU'RE USING HIM AS A SHIELD AGAIN?!
YOU'RE HURTING HIM!
URRGGH
TOMNYAN I NEED YOU TO GET RID OF HER WITH-OUT USING FORCE!
!!!
SH
WHAT?! THAT HUMAN'S PROTECT-ING ME?!
IT'S SUP-POSE TO BE ME, ISN'T IT?
I CAN'T SLOW DOWN!
CHOOM
CHOOM
CHOOM
CHOOM
AGGGGH!

!!!
SHOOF
CHOOM
CHOOM
CHOOM
CHOOM
CHOOM
ARRRRRRRGH!
I REPAID YOU... BECAUSE ...
...YOU PRO-TECTED ME FIRST! ♪
I...THINK SO... THANKS...
ARE... ARE YOU OKAY...?

THUNGK
THAT WAS REALLY CLOSE!
HEY! SHE STILL BLOCKED THE ATTACK WITH WHISPER!
STARE
IT WAS HER FAULT...
HOW COULD YOU DO SUCH A THING?
I'M SORRY...
...
NNGH
WHISPER, ARE YOU OKAY?

YOU DON'T ONLY ASK FOR KICKBACKS, DO YOU? YOU ALSO REPAY PEOPLE!
OF COURSE!
BUT...IT WAS ME... THAT HELPED YOU...!
HELPING OTHERS IS ONLY NATURAL...
...AND SO IS PAYING THEM BACK WHEN THEY HELP YOU! ♪
I THOUGHT SHE ONLY EVER ASKED FOR THINGS AND NEVER HELPED OUT...
HAHAHA
ANYWAY, SINCE I JUST HELPED YOU...
...GIMME SOME-THING IN RETURN!
SHE REALLY STICKS TO HER PLANS...
WELL... WHAT DO YOU WANT?

WHAT?
FOR YOU TO BE MY FRIEND! ♪

NO IT'S NOT!
THAT'S SO SELF-SERVING!
...

HEE HEE HEE.
I FIGURE EVERY TIME YOU SUMMON ME...
...YOU'LL END UP GIVING ME SOMETHING! ♪

BUT ASKING PEOPLE FOR KICKBACKS ALL THE TIME...
...AND I ALWAYS THINK ABOUT ASKING THEM FOR HELP LATER!
I'VE BEFRIENDED A LOT OF YO-KAI...

FRIENDS SHOULD ALWAYS THANK EACH OTHER PROPERLY.
GIVE AND TAKE IS NATURAL IN A FRIENDSHIP! ♪ RIGHT?
...
BAAM
WHY ARE YOU OKAY WITH THIS?! FRIENDS SHOULDN'T USE EACH OTHER AS SHIELDS!!!
HA HA. ♪ NICE TO MEET YOU!
YOU TOO! ♪
WHY AREN'T YOU LISTENING TO ME?!
ARRRRRRG!!

NATE ADAMS'S CURRENT NUMBER OF YO-KAI FRIENDS: 74

I THINK IT'S ABOUT TIME...
...THAT WE HAD A TALK.
BA
A
I...

-GHOULFATHER ARC BEGINNING IN THE NEXT VOLUME!!

Little Battlers eXperience

LBX
LITTLE BATTLERS EXPERIENCE

Story and Art by
HIDEAKI FUJII

Welcome to the world of Little Battlers eXperience! In the near future, a boy named Van Yamano owns Achilles, a miniaturized robot that battles on command! But Achilles is no ordinary LBX. Hidden inside him is secret data that Van must keep out of the hands of evil at all costs!

All six volumes available now!

DANBALL SENKI
© 2011 Hideaki FUJII / SHOGAKUKAN
©LEVEL-5 Inc.

RATED A ALL AGES
ratings.viz.com

viz media
www.viz.com

PERFECT SQUARE
www.perfectsquare.com

Welcome to the world of Little Battlers eXperience! In the near future, a boy named Van Yamano owns Achilles, a miniaturized robot that battles on command! But Achilles is no ordinary LBX. Hidden inside him is secret data that Van must keep out of the hands of evil at all costs!

Little Battlers eXperience

Story and Art by
HIDEAKI FUJII

APPEARANCE

AH!
COULD IT BE ...?!
I HAVEN'T BEEN APPEARING IN THE MANGA RECENTLY ...

SHOOCK
HA HA HA. ♪ THAT'S POSSI-BLE. ♪
HUMPH.
MAYBE THE AUTHOR HAS GOTTEN BORED OF ME?!

PFFFT. RIGHT. ♪
HUUH ?!
SHOOK
LOOK WHO'S TALKING! YOU'VE HAD EVEN LESS APPEAR-ANCES THAN ME!!
HUMPH.

TOM-NYAN PLAYS A MAJOR ROLE IN VOLUME 13.
DON'T GIVE ME THAT LOOK OF PITY!
UH-HUH...
VEEEEN
...
E-EH, TH-THAT'S OKAY.

AUTHOR BIO

A kid I signed an autograph for during my *Go-Go-Go Saiyuki* days is my new assistant. I'm not musing about how quickly time moves though. I'm just saying… All nine volumes of *Go-Go-Go Saiyuki* are available now in Japan! You can also get them digitally!
—Noriyuki Konishi

Noriyuki Konishi hails from Shimabara City in Nagasaki Prefecture, Japan. He debuted with the one-shot *E-CUFF* in *Monthly Shonen Jump Original* in 1997. He is known in Japan for writing manga adaptations of *AM Driver* and *Mushiking: King of the Beetles*, along with *Saiyuki Hiro Go-Kū Den!*, *Chōhenshin Gag Gaiden!! Card Warrior Kamen Riders*, *Go-Go-Go Saiyuki: Shin Gokūden* and more. Konishi was the recipient of the 38th Kodansha manga award in 2014 and the 60th Shogakukan manga award in 2015.

FORT WORTH PUBLIC LIBRARY
31668074173318

THIS IS THE END OF THIS GRAPHIC NOVEL!

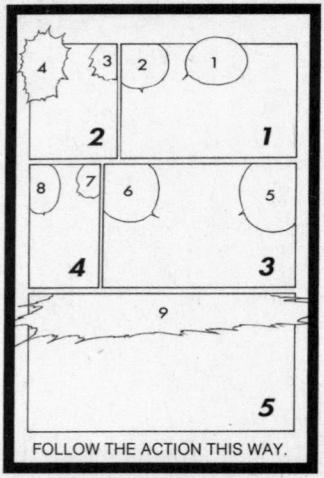

To properly enjoy this graphic novel, please turn it around and begin reading from right to left.